Watch Out, Sara!

Anna Sellberg

Watch Out, Sara!

ISBN: 1-933343-35-4

Stabenfeldt, Inc.
457 North Main Street
Danbury, CT 06811
www.pony.us

Chapter 1

The afternoon sun was broiling us as we worked under the clear blue sky. The air close to the surface of the riding course shimmered in the heat and it made horses and riders pant and sweat.

I shortened my reins and started to gallop. Fandango snorted and tried to buck, but I pulled him in and managed to keep him focused and calm. He threw his head impatiently when we came to three parallel oxers on the middle track, all spread three-and-a-half feet apart. They weren't high, but with their width they demanded both strength and concentration in order to get over all three without losing rhythm or missing one. After we took those three, we turned left and went right over a vertical fence jump, and then took a few more jumps before the course ended.

Fandango cleared all the obstacles without a second's hesitation – all I needed to do was sit tight in the saddle until our riding instructor finally was satisfied.

"Great job, Sara. You can slow down now and let him walk around with long reins. Now it's your turn, Kate!"

I slowed Fandango to a walk and patted his neck. He was dripping with sweat, and so was I. My mouth felt as dry as a desert, my eyes hurt with all the dust from the track, and sweat ran down my face in streaks. In other words, I was a mess!

I let Fandango lope along with neck reins while I looked around the course and fields. It had been a tough lesson, but it was exactly what we needed after the long summer off with very little formal training.

There were four of us: three active riders and a fourth who was standing by the fence chatting. Kate was the oldest. She was almost eighteen, and this would be her last year competing with her white Connemara, Max. He was just 56 inches high, jumped like a cat, and they had won lots of prizes as a team over the years.

The other rider was a tiny blonde girl whom I'd never seen before. Her name was Molly, and she rode a brown, long-legged horse that didn't look like a pony, although he was exactly the same height as Fandango. While Kate and Max flew over the obstacles like experts, the girl trotted around on a small course further from the riding ring. She seemed nervous, and her horse didn't obey her commands very well. I knew that Josie was having them go last in order to give Molly a little extra help. Josie is absolutely the world's best riding instructor. She always makes sure that everyone gets something from every lesson. No matter how down and grouchy you are when the lesson starts, you're always in a great mood after. It's because she is so unbelievably positive and manages to bring out the best in both the rider and the horse.

I heard a flirtatious giggle and glanced over at the fourth

rider leaning nonchalantly on the fence. It was Fredrik. He was already finished with his lesson, and he let a young girl with brown hair ride his pony, "Busy Bee," while he stood and chatted with a couple of the female stable hands. He had a soda can in his hand that he drank from while the girls watched him with awe. Fredrik boards his pony at the riding school, and the stable girls fight over who gets to help him with his pony. Fredrik's handsome, (at least he thinks he is!) and he uses his good looks to the max in order to get the girls to do the boring chores, like leading Busy Bee around to cool down after the lesson and mucking out the stall. I hate Fredrik and he hates me, and our relationship didn't get any better after he'd had to leave Busy Bee with my family for a few weeks over the summer.

We usually try to avoid each other as much as possible, and when I can, I go out of my way to do so. Unfortunately, we see each other at school every day, even though we go to a big high school. He manages to choose almost the same subjects as I and, day in and day out, I'm forced to see his smug grin and listen to his drawling voice.

I sighed and rode through the gate. On the way to our car I met Fredrik's father, Frank, who had a thin, expensive sweat blanket over his arm. I avoided making eye contact. It seems impossible, but I dislike his father even more than I dislike Fredrik. Earlier in the summer my boyfriend Mike, my younger sister Sophia, and I discovered that he was doing something horrible – he had bought a bunch of stolen horses and planned to sell them. While the horses were in his care, he had built a large aluminum box-like structure in the middle of the woods to contain them. The truck driver didn't give the horses any food or water, and when we finally discovered them, several were exhausted and several more were dying. That's why I hate him.

My mom waited for Fandango and me by the car. She had filled a bucket with water, and as soon as I removed Fandango's saddle she began to sponge him off. Fandango enjoyed the cool water, and soon began to nip at the grass tufts that grew here and there in the gravel stable yard.

I took off my helmet and fluffed out my medium-length blonde hair. I was soaking with sweat, and the dust from the riding track grated between my teeth.

"There's a bottle of orange juice in the car, if you're thirsty," Mom said. "Sit and drink while I take care of Fandango."

"Thanks," I said as I took one. The juice was quite warm since it had been in the hot car for almost two hours, but I still emptied the bottle in one big swig. It tasted so good!

I looked toward the track where the blonde girl had just steered toward a low cross with a ramp in front of it. The girl and her horse went toward the obstacle with a pace that was a cross between a trot and a gallop. The horse stumbled over the ramp and was at the point of continuing forward when he put his nose right through the little cross. It was a miracle, but both horse and rider made it over and continued in a jerking trot. Suddenly a flash went off in my head – the horse was a Standardbred pacer! I didn't know why I hadn't realized it before. Many pacers aren't taller than fifty-nine inches, which is the maximum height for a pony, so this was a small pacer.

I watched while the girl jumped. Sometimes the horse made a very fine jump, like a helicopter – right up and right down, with the girl helplessly hanging onto the reins.

Somehow, as if by magic, Josie finally made order out of the horse and rider, and they worked together much better as a team.

"C'mon now," Josie shouted, "let's get together to talk about today's lesson."

Fredrik, Kate and I went over to her while the new girl got off her horse and gave the reins to a tall, skinny man who must have been about 60 years old. He looked worn out, was unshaved, and had a few gray hairs sticking out from under his cap. I know I shouldn't judge people by their looks, but he really didn't look very friendly or well kept.

"I think you all showed great ability today," Josie said, looking very happy. "Kate, just remember that even if Max is experienced, he still needs help sometimes so that he doesn't make an error by going too fast. Fredrik – you must continue to practice more with flat work, and you too, Sara," she said, talking to me. "By the way, have either of you been in a dressage ring with your horses this summer?"

Fredrik rolled his eyes and I sucked in a deep breath. Dressage has never exactly been my strong point, and both Dad and Josie get after me all the time about training more.

"And you, Molly," Josie said last, "you should continue to jump low obstacles and trot over cavaletti. I know that both you and your horse can learn to jump, but your horse must learn to understand your signals with certainty so he knows what you expect him to do."

Josie smiled at us.

"Okay, we'll see you next week. Please help take apart and put away all the obstacles," she said.

She nodded good-bye as she strode with long steps toward the riding school's stable while we riders began to break down all the obstacles we had set up for the lesson.

"What sort of horse is that?" Kate asked in a friendly manner while we each struggled with our vertical obstacle. Molly responded with a shy look and said he was a Standardbred and his name was "Little Brother."

"He really can jump, but we have to learn more technique, which is why I'm training him," she said quietly. Fredrik was not the type to let something like that go by without an insult.

"Maybe you should take lessons on how to gallop too," he said with a malicious grin. "Old pacers usually need to learn that!"

"Oh, stop it, Fredrik," Kate said. "That wasn't necessary."

Fredrik shrugged his shoulders in a "who cares" gesture.

"I don't understand why you'd want to ride a pacer when there are so many real riding horses," he said. "Pacers belong on pacer tracks – or as lunchmeat!"

"Turning horses into lunchmeat is something you have a lot of experience with!" I rebuked him.

Fredrik gave me a dirty look and stormed off with his lips pressed together in a scowl and his nose in the air.

The new girl looked nervous, Kate laughed and I felt satisfied that I'd scored a bull's-eye with the sarcastic Fredrik. On the other hand, it wasn't particularly difficult, after what Fredrik's dad had done earlier in the summer.

Outside the riding ring, Fandango was enjoying the green grass while my mom put his leg wrappings on for the ride home.

"Are you ready, Sara?" she called and I nodded.

"Great, then let's go home," she said as she led Fandango to the trailer.

She led him right in while I fastened the boom and shut the gate. Fandango began to eat the hay out of the hay net in front of him. He is a real chowhound, and no matter how much he takes in, there's always room for more!

Right beside us in the parking lot was a little horse trailer with room for two horses, and Molly was loading her horse. The tall gray-haired man held her saddle and bridle in his arms. When Molly's eyes met mine, she smiled shyly and nodded.

"Who's that?" Mom asked. "I haven't seen her at any lessons before."

"She's a new girl named Molly," I said. "She rides a Standardbred pacer."

"Hmmm," Mom said thinking, "I wonder of she belongs to the people who moved into the Hancock's farm up on the ridge? It's been for sale for a long time, and I heard that some harness racing folks had bought it."

"Possibly," I said and took out my cell phone. The text message symbol was blinking and I smiled, as I was sure it was from my boyfriend, Mike.

But no, it was just from my little sister, Sophia. Darn!

Can u pick me up Alexandra's ASAP? Flat tire! she'd written. Mom nodded.

"Okay," Mom said. "Call her and say we'll be there in 15 minutes."

I made the call and then sat back, quietly staring out the window. I couldn't help but be disappointed that it wasn't Mike who'd called. Mike works as a horse caretaker on a farm that belongs to our neighbors Hans and Maggie, and we'd been dating for almost three months. It's been the most wonderful time of my life, and I like Mike more than anything! But for a while now I've had a feeling that things aren't as great between us as they were. It's hard to explain, but it feels as if he doesn't care about me as much any more. For example, he doesn't call me that much. And it's been a while since we've done anything together. It's true that he and Hans have been working overtime building a new barn, but it's almost finished. Hans's old barn burned down at the beginning of the summer, and it's been a rush job trying to finish it before fall, which my brain understands. But my heart thinks that Mike must at least have *some* free time to call!

We finally arrived at Sophia's best friend's house and my sister hopped in the car. Her bike was leaning against a tree in their yard, and I asked her why she didn't put it in the horse trailer.

"Martin, a friend of Alexandra's brother, promised to fix it for me!" my boy-crazy little sister said with glee. She waved to Alexandra, who stood on the front steps, while Mom restarted the car.

"Were you riding?" Sophia asked and I nodded. She wrinkled her nose in disgust.

"I can smell it," she said. "I don't understand why you want to ride all the time!"

I shrugged my shoulders.

Sophia and I are as different as two sisters can be. Sophia is tall and light blonde with looks that would make a fashion model jealous. I'm a few inches shorter, and my dark blonde hair will never grow that long or be that thick, so mostly I get it cut short or wear it in a pony tail.

Sophia loves everything to do with fashion, clothes and jewelry, and does everything she can to attract guys, which isn't hard. They fly to her like bees to a sugared drink glass on a warm summer day. And guys are practically the only things she thinks and talks about. Boring! I care mostly about horses. I would never buy a bunch of expensive clothes when I could, for example, buy a new blanket or ribbons for one of my horses.

A few years ago Sophia loved horses as much as I do, but several months ago she suddenly lost interest in them, and now Camigo, my old show pony that she inherited, just hangs out in the pasture and has a quiet, restful life. It's unfortunate for him, because he loves to compete. Sophia used to ride him occasionally, but now she's totally outgrown him. I get the feeling that Camigo will live out his days in the pasture, with nothing meaningful to do. Of course, I ride him a few times a week so he gets some exercise, but it's not nearly enough.

We stopped in our driveway where I unloaded Fandango, who went nicely into the barn and ate his grain while I unloaded the saddle, bridle and everything else in the car. I then let him out into the pasture, and was so happy watching how he went to join the other three horses – Camigo, Dad's old show horse Maverick, and my new show horse Winny.

Fandango went right over to a particularly dusty place right inside the gate and, with a dramatic groan, sunk to the ground and rolled around and around.

In spite of the fact that I was still in a bad mood because Mike hadn't called, I couldn't help but smile, and I was still smiling while I walked to the house to take a long, cool shower.

Chapter 2

The screeching alarm clock woke me from a deep sleep. I had promised Dad that I would take care of the horses while he and Mom slept in, since they'd been to a party the night before.

It was a sunny day, the sky was clear blue without a cloud in sight, and it felt more like summer than fall. When I stepped into the stable, Fandango started kicking his stall door. He does this all the time to remind us not to forget to give him his breakfast. He obviously thinks he's dangerously close to starving to death.

I fed him first and then I gave Camigo, Maverick and Winny their food. Then I put them out in the summer pasture where there was still good grass for grazing.

When I finished with the horses, I went in again and grabbed a glass of juice and a bowl of cereal. The rest of the family was still sleeping, so I took my breakfast up to my room. Mom and Dad had come home late, and Sophia never woke up before noon on Saturdays.

I smiled to myself when I thought about my own

Friday night. After I'd showered, Mike had called, and he was actually free to go out – for once! We went into town and ate at a small pizzeria, and then went to a club where we met up with a bunch of friends. We had a great time, and all my thoughts about our relationship being on the rocks had blown away like the wind.

I yawned and opened the thick book that I had just started to read. It was a love story that took place during World War II. Even though it was exciting, I had a hard time keeping my eyes open. I soon realized that I had two choices – either lie down and try to go back to sleep, or go do something that required exercise.

Exercise won out – I decided to go for a ride. It was a beautiful day, and Fandango would love a ride through the woods after our difficult training yesterday. I put Josie's suggestion that Fandango and I practice dressage every day until next Friday completely out of my mind. We were going to have fun!

A short time later, Fandango and I ambled out of the yard. He seemed just as energetic and happy as always, and strode with long steps. I had no plan to go in any particular direction. There are a bunch of great riding trails, small roads and paths around our farm, and we had ridden most of them about a million times.

Suddenly I had an idea – why not ride up and see if it was Molly's family that had moved into the Hancock's old farm?

I turned Fandango into the small wooded trail that I knew went in that direction. As soon as we were in the woods, I shortened the reins and he began to trot. It was a good distance to the Ridge Farm, as the old Hancock farm was called, but I felt up for a long ride in this wonderful weather.

It had been an eternity since I last rode out this way, but I soon found the path, and it wasn't as far as I thought. First we followed a little path through the woods, and then we came to a gravel path where we could gallop. Eventually the gravel path turned into a gravel road and I knew exactly where I was and how to get to their farm. The road curved up toward the ridge's crown, and I guided Fandango into a slow gallop. There was hardly any traffic, and on a straight stretch I allowed Fandango to increase his speed. The wind felt cool against my face as his hooves pounded the gravel road. I was so happy and thought to myself that no one could be happier!

At that moment a pacer pulling a rider in a cart came around the curve at full speed, and I was rudely awakened from my daydreams. Fandango was frightened, and he stopped dead in his tracks so quickly that I had no hope of staying on his back! I flew over his head like a projectile – but by pure luck I managed to turn around in midair and land on my feet, still holding the reins!

The pacer didn't even slow down, even though he must have seen me fly off the horse. Instead he continued to come at us at top speed, quickly coming nearer and nearer. Fandango snorted and ran around me once and hopped into the ditch. He stood there snorting, more like a fire-spitting dragon than a horse. I expected him to try to take control of the reins, turn around and run home without me!

Anger made me turn toward the pacer and scream, *"Why don't you stop?"* Finally the driver reined in the large brown horse to a nice, slow walk.

"Haven't you ever seen a pacer before?" the driver asked sarcastically when they were close to us, and I had the feeling that he thought it was funny that Fandango had been frightened.

When he spoke, I recognized the face under the dirty cap. It was the gray-haired man who was with Molly the day before! I wondered if the man could be her grandfather, because he looked much older than sixty.

"We don't have very many pacers around here," I tried to sound friendly while I calmly patted Fandango on the neck.

"Really – then he'll have to get used to them from now on," the old man said, dismissing me, and a second later he whipped the horse forward again and went trotting by, disappearing down the road.

Fandango snorted his frustration and took a few side steps before I succeeded in calming him down and getting him to jump up on the road again. It was useless for me to try to get up on the saddle. Fandango just ran around and around, and I couldn't even get my foot in the stirrup. Finally I led him to a spot with lots of green grass and small bushes by the side of the road, and while he took a few chomps I was able to get myself into the saddle.

"Inconsiderate jerk," I spat out to no one in particular as I shortened the reins. "He could have at least waited for Fandango to calm down, before he took off with his horse again."

I was still shaking with rage, and I had the feeling that he'd scared Fandango on purpose. Or was it just my imagination? I didn't know, and I tried to shake off these unpleasant thoughts by letting Fandango trot again. He seemed tense, and jumped at all the small things that wouldn't have bothered him if the pacer hadn't come by.

When we came up to the top of the ridge the woods opened up, and there was Ridge Farm. I hadn't been there in a while, and the place had really changed! In the big pasture along the road where the Hancocks used to have their cows, three brown Standardbreds were grazing, and the rusty old barbed wire had been replaced with attractive white rough wood thin planks and electric wire. A little further away, a short, blond man stood pounding a stake in the ground, and it looked like he was building another pasture. He nodded and greeted me in a friendly manner as I rode by.

For the most part, I didn't see another person anywhere. I looked in the yard, which was almost deserted, except for a tiger cat that sat in the barn door like he was guarding the whole place.

I was just going to turn Fandango around and ride toward the blond man and ask for Molly when I heard someone call my name.

I turned around with surprise as I heard my name again. Then I saw Molly waving happily from a window on the second floor of the farmhouse.

As I was reining in Fandango, Molly came running out to the yard.

"Hi!" she shouted, and then became very shy. "Oh … I didn't know you lived nearby."

"It's not exactly the next farm over," I said, "but I wanted a long ride, and I decided to come over and see if it was true that you lived here."

"Awesome," Molly said, petting Fandango's neck.

"We've only lived here for a few weeks, and I don't know much about the area. I don't know where you live."

I told here where our farm is, and she nodded, although I could tell that she didn't really know where I was talking about.

"We aren't from around here," she said, and it sounded almost like an apology. "Little Brother and I haven't had time to ride any of the trails around here yet."

"Why's he called Little Brother?" I asked, and Molly grinned again.

"Because he *is* a little brother! His mom had twins, and he was the smaller and younger of the two. He was so tiny that we had to feed him with a baby bottle in the beginning. I slept in the stable every night, and we all helped with him. Later my mom and dad gave him to me. Do you want to see the stable?" she asked, and I nodded.

"Sure, but what should I do with Fandango while we're over there?"

"My dad's just finished building a little paddock. Do you think he'll be okay in there?"

I said that would be fine and dismounted, and we walked together into the yard. This little paddock was built with the same white rough wood thin planks. I silently prayed that Fandango wouldn't gnaw on the ends of the fine newly painted fence. He loves to scratch himself too, and the fence looked very tempting with its rough wood.

After we put Fandango in the paddock and gave him a little hay that we'd brought down from the loft, Molly showed me around. The cowshed, where the Hancocks had kept their thirty milking cows, had been rebuilt into a stable. At this point there weren't very many stalls, but

Molly explained that they planned to build enough stalls for fifteen horses.

"After the stalls are done, we plan to build our own racetrack where we can train the horses and then, of course, several more paddocks. And maybe we'll build a riding ring, too," said Molly, and she patted Little Brother as we stood by the pasture where he was hanging out with the other horses. "But we'll see … Daddy's not exactly happy that I ride horseback. He wants me to be a harness driver and follow in his footsteps."

At that point I thought the unpleasant gray-haired man must be her father, even though he seemed way too old to have such a young daughter. He'd looked really angry during the lesson yesterday, and I thought he should have been proud that Molly was improving, even though it was jumping and not trotting.

"Why doesn't Little Brother compete in the harness races?" I asked, and Molly shook her head and grinned.

"He's way too slow. He has no instinct for winning, none at all! So I get to ride him instead, and I've always dreamed of jumping."

Little Brother nuzzled me in a friendly way, and I patted him on his head. He was brown, like most Standardbreds, with a little star in the middle of his forehead and white stripes on his sides. His head was long and his neck was narrow, and even though his facial expression was sad he looked really handsome. After we left the pasture, he stood at the fence and watched us for a few minutes before he began to graze again.

We went over to Fandango who was standing half asleep in the paddock. I noticed that he hadn't rubbed himself against the new fence, which made me happy. What luck!

"Well," I said, "I should get going now."

"Okay … Or would you like a snack first?" Molly asked, suddenly sounding shy again. "Or maybe you're not hungry, or don't have time?"

"Oh, sure," I said, "I can! First thing, though, I should call my parents and tell them where I am!"

I used my cell phone to call, and then we went to the pretty red main farmhouse.

It was cluttered inside, with moving boxes everywhere. Molly's mom was in the kitchen putting dishes, pots and pans and utensils in drawers and cabinets. She was short and plump, with long dark hair and the same brown eyes that Molly had. She gave me a big smile and Molly introduced us. Her mother's name was Jane Peters. We exchanged greetings while Molly was getting out juice and cookies.

Then Molly and I went out on the porch and talked about horses for a long time. The time just flew by.

Molly and I were the same age, and I wondered why I hadn't seen her at school since we should be in the same class. Molly told me that she hadn't started school yet. She'd had a really bad case of the flu at the beginning of the semester, and had been stuck in bed for almost two weeks.

An hour and a half later, we went down to the stable yard where Fandango was looking for grass stalks in the paddock's gravel. I saddled and bridled him while Molly hung on the fence, chatting with me. All her shyness was gone, and it felt like we'd been friends forever.

The blond man who'd been building the fence earlier came over to us carrying his toolbox and said hello to me.

"This is my Dad, Erik Peters," Molly said as an introduction.

"Hi, I'm Sara," I said, and was so glad that the gray-haired man wasn't her dad. Molly's dad was much nicer!

"Can you throw down some hay and feed the horses?" Erik asked, and Molly nodded.

"I'll help too," I said, and Erik nodded to me.

"Great. We've got so much to do to get the stalls finished before it turns cold. Then we've got to hurry and build a fence before our first boarders arrive in a few weeks," Erik sighed, but I could tell by his tone that he was very pleased with everything.

Molly smiled at him as he went into the house.

"Living like this and taking care of horses is our dream," she said as she turned toward me. "Mom and Dad have talked and planned for years, and now their dream's finally come true. I can hardly believe it myself. Sometimes I wake up in the morning and pinch myself in the arm to make sure I haven't just dreamt the whole thing!"

"You'll get used to it soon," I grinned, and then teased. "Wait 'til it's winter, when we've got to plow you out from your yard, the car gets stuck on the hill, the water in the barn freezes, and you've got a power outage because a bunch of trees fell on the lines in the last storm."

"Oh, no," Molly said laughing, "We can handle it, if that's all!"

We climbed up to the huge hayloft. It was about two-thirds full, with bales of green hay. It went all the way to the ceiling where the sun shone in through some small windows high up on the short sides. The dust danced in the sunshine, and it smelled like summer.

"Look, there's that cat!" Molly suddenly cried out as she pointed toward a corner of the hay.

"Where?" I looked surprised. "I don't see a cat!"

"She went between the bales," Molly said. "She's really skittish, almost like a feral cat, I think. When I saw her last week she had a really round tummy, but now she looks thin … I wonder if she's hidden a litter of kittens up here someplace?"

"C'mon," I said, "let's try to find them. If the mother cat's wild, it's best if we find the kittens and try to tame them early, or they'll be wild too."

We went around the loft and searched for the cat, but of course we didn't have any luck. We moved a couple of bales away from the wall at the spot where the cat had disappeared through a small narrow opening between the bales, but we didn't catch a glimpse of cat or kittens.

"I'll go get a little cat food and a water bowl," Molly said. "If I put them up here, she's sure to come out to eat in a while."

"Good idea," I nodded, and at that moment we heard someone climbing up the small wooden steps to the loft. A second later, the tall, gray-haired man, the man who'd driven the pacer on the road and scared Fandango, appeared! He stared at me, and I knew that he recognized me. His look was piercing and unpleasant – and I wasn't sure, but it seemed that a look of fear flashed across his face when he first saw me!

"What in blazes are you two doing up here?" he spat out with so much anger that both Molly and I instinctively took a step backwards.

"We're throwing hay down to feed the horses," Molly said, trying to sound brave. "Dad asked us to do it."

23

The man took a quick look at his watch.

"Get a move on, then! You're almost twenty minutes late feeding them."

"We were looking for a cat," I said, and tried to cheer him up by being polite. "We think she's hidden a litter of kittens up here in the hay. She went in there between the bales, so we moved them to look for her, and the –"

"There are no cats here," the gray haired man snarled angrily. "And you have no business nosing around in the hay! You wreck the bales if you move them around! Now get out of here. I'll feed the horses."

"But my dad said that –" Molly began, but the man shouted at her before she could finish.

"I said get lost. It's better that I feed them, so it gets done."

The man almost roared the last bit. He was bright red in the face, and stared at us with watery blood-red eyes, looking as if he'd like to use his fists on us to show how serious he was.

"Okay, then," Molly said, trying to sound completely friendly, even though I could hear her voice shaking. "We're going. I'll go tell my dad that you –"

He muttered something that I couldn't hear, then went over to the nearest pile of hay bales and began to throw them down.

We hurried down the steep ladder. I felt so relieved to be down and away from his threatening, hateful manner. I couldn't help wonder why he was so angry! I knew that Molly's dad had hired him – but why would he hire someone who acted like that? I couldn't understand it ... Molly and I hadn't exactly made a mess of the hayloft.

24

We'd just moved a few bales to one side that we would have put back again. Nothing more …

It was time to ride home, and I saddled Fandango while Molly leaned on the fence and watched. Neither of us said anything, and I think we both felt a little embarrassed about what had happened.

"I hope you don't mind my asking," I said finally after getting on Fandango, "but who is he, exactly?"

Molly snuck a look at the barn.

"He's George, our horse hand. But you'd better get going. We'll talk in school!"

I rode out of the courtyard, and after a few steps I turned and waved, but Molly didn't wave back. Instead I saw her run into the farmhouse without looking back – and I couldn't help the very uncomfortable feeling growing in my gut.

Chapter 3

The next day Molly and I met in the cafeteria during our lunch period. Since both of my horses needed a rest day, we decided to go over to her house again. At first, I thought about saying no because of what happened with George the day before. But at the same time, I couldn't help but be a little bit curious about the strange old man. I thought about asking Molly about him while we were eating, but never go the chance as we were hanging out with three gabby girls, and then we didn't have any more classes together that afternoon.

After school both of us got out to the pick-up site early and waited for Molly's mom. She'd been to the farm store, and the back of the van was filled with large rolls of electric wire, fencing pieces and other stuff.

"We have to build new pastures and paddocks," Molly explained as the car turned onto the large roadway that led toward their house. "There was a ton of fencing, but since the farm was unoccupied for so long, folks just came by and helped themselves to fence posts, wire, whatever!" she continued.

"True, but there was just barbed wire fencing around the pastures," Jane said. "Barbed wire isn't good for horses – they should have electric fences with wooden posts and rails."

"Or that really nice white fencing," Molly said, and her mom just smiled.

"We won't have anywhere near that amount of money for a long time for a fence like that. Not even if Black Babe keeps winning for many years to come."

Molly's dad was unloading a huge load of straw. George was nowhere to be seen, so we offered to help.

It went quickly, getting all the straw into the loft, but carrying the huge bales was heavy work, and it made us all sweaty. I had straw all over me, prickly small pieces of straw that itched and irritated my skin.

When we were finally finished, Molly's dad wiped the sweat from his brow and smiled at us.

"Thanks, girls," he said. " I have no idea where George is. He should've been here hours ago."

"Where do you suppose he went?" Molly asked, and she gazed toward the little cottage where George lived.

"He went to town earlier to have his computer fixed, and I gave him a few hours to look around, as I didn't have any idea how long it would take to fix. Well, I should get back to work. See you later, girls!"

Eric went out and Molly and I each sighed and sank down on our own bale of hay. I looked around the huge loft. The hay was as neatly stacked as it was before. After we had packed in the straw, the whole loft was almost crammed. By the stairs two dishes, one with cat food and the other with water, made me remember the cat that Molly had spoken about the day before.

27

"Have you seen that cat?" I asked, and Molly nodded.

"Yeah, but not the kittens. I waited very quietly for her to come eat last night, and when she thought no one was here she showed up. I'm sure she has her kittens somewhere! Mom and Dad think so too. I want to try to tame the kittens."

"I wonder why George got so mad when we were up here yesterday?" I asked. "Your dad asked us to feed the horses. He should've been glad that we were helping him!"

"George is nuts," Molly said with a sigh. "He's always been a really strange person, and no one can figure him out. But lately he's become much worse. For example, he's always angry with me whenever I'm in the stable. No matter what I say, he's mean to me. And I am forbidden to feed, muck out, or do anything with the horses – except brush and ride Little Brother. 'I'll do it all,' he says. It doesn't matter that I think it's fun to help out in the stable!"

"Did you tell your parents?" I asked, and Molly nodded.

"I've tried, but it doesn't help. Mom says that I should talk with Dad, and Dad says that I should leave George alone and stop pestering him –"

"Stop pestering him?" I interrupted, "It's the other way around – he's after you all the time."

"Well," Molly said as an afterthought. "I think Dad had to offer him a job. He didn't have one, and besides, he works for almost nothing, plus he takes excellent care of Black Babe."

"Black Babe?" I questioned. "I don't know anything about harness racing, but the name sounds familiar. Isn't he really famous?"

Molly began to chuckle. I don't know what I said that was so funny, and I had no idea whose horse he was.

"Black Babe's the biggest winning mare for all of last year. She almost broke a world's record for mares, and if she hadn't gone lame right before the start, she would have won the Little Brown Jug Race. She's incredibly fast – unlike her little brother, who can't run at all," Molly said with a broad grin.

I thought about a harness race that I had seen on TV not too long ago. In the home stretch, a long legged black horse came from behind at full speed, easily went around the lead horse and won the race by two lengths. The TV commentator was in ecstasy and kept shouting about a world's record. *That* was Black Babe!

"And that's why I ride Little Brother instead of her. He's a total washout in front of a sulky."

I stared a Molly while it slowly dawned on me what she'd said.

"Are Black Babe and Little Brother siblings?"

"Yup," Molly said, "they're twins! Didn't I tell you that before? No one thought either horse would make it, since twin foals are usually small and no one wants them. But Black Babe is the best there is! And all the money she's won meant that we could buy this farm and move here."

"That's amazing," I said. "How exciting for you!"

"It was a given that we'd hire George! He's cared for Black Babe since she was a filly and began training with one of my dad's buddies. Back then George was incredibly wonderful with horses, and he was on the way to becoming a first-rate driver. But then it all went out the window for him. He got addicted to gambling and lost his farm and his horses, but that was a long time ago."

"Oh …" I said.

"No matter what anyone did, Black Babe wouldn't run for anyone but George. She was as fast as all get out, but no one could train her before George started taking care of her and training her his way. Without him, Black Babe would be nothing. And that's why dad's so grateful to George and keeps him around."

I nodded. It wasn't really so difficult to understand. A pacer who wouldn't trot to win wasn't worth any money, but Black Babe, who'd won one championship race after another, was worth millions!

"A few months ago, Black Babe won a huge race and tons of money. Right after that I know that George borrowed money from dad – a *lot* of money – to pay off his gambling debts. To repay Dad, George agreed to move here and work for a while, till Mom and Dad built up the business. He works for almost nothing in order to pay back his loan."

"Well," I said, stretching. "Let's get going. We've got things to do."

"Let's go driving on the track," Molly said when we reached the stable floor.

"Awesome!" I said. "I've never driven a pacer!"

"It's so much fun," Molly said as she took a halter that was hanging on a hook outside of Little Brother's stall. "I'll get Little Brother, and then we have to hurry before it gets dark."

Molly disappeared, heading out to the pasture, and I got the riding gear that was hanging outside Little Brother's stall. Out of the corner of my eye I saw a movement that made me turn around quickly, and a few yards behind me in the passageway stood George with his arms crossed over his chest. He gave me a look that made me cold with fear. How long had he been in the barn, I wondered? Had he heard Molly and me talking about him when we were up in the loft? The idea didn't sit well.

I was able to swallow my fear and nod at him and say, "hi," as if he were any old person I would greet. Luck was with me, because at that moment Molly came into the barn with Little Brother. George gave a snort and slowly went into his office at the other end of the barn. He slammed the door behind him.

"Yikes, that was scary!" I whispered to Molly, and she understood.

"Do you think he heard us talking about him?" I whispered as Molly shot a sideways glance at his office door.

"I don't know," she said, "but he has begun to sneak around. Sometimes I have no idea that he's there until suddenly he's standing next to me with an angry look on his face."

I nodded and shot a glance toward the closed door, wishing that I hadn't come home with Molly.

Little Brother had a blanket on when he was out in the pasture, so even though he'd rolled around in the mud, he wasn't all that dirty. He stood nice and still while I helped Molly brush him. We both worked quickly, even though we'd never talked about who was going to do what. We just wanted to get out of there fast.

Molly harnessed him and attached him to a red shaft. The harness was small and tight and had several different strands that had to be twisted, stretched and fastened in a variety of ways. Molly did it quickly, as if by instinct, while I stood by and watched – totally dumbfounded.

"How do you possibly know how to put all this stuff on him correctly?" I asked after she'd finished fastening him to the sulky, which he pulled toward the stable door.

"I dunno," Molly said and shrugged her shoulders. "It's not hard – in fact it's really pretty logical."

We each took a helmet from the saddle room and jumped up in the sulky. Molly sat on the right and drove and I sat beside her. Little Brother walked with a slow yet eager pace out of the stable yard. Molly talked to him calmly, and I just sat and worried about what would happen if he decided to kick back with his long hind legs.

"We're so unprotected, sitting here," I said with an uneasy feeling. "What if he decides to kick us?"

"You'll get used to it," Molly said smiling, and she smacked Little Brother, who began to trot at a normal pace. Molly held the reins steady while she glanced back at me.

"Is this too fast for you?" she teased, grinning. "We can slow down again if you want."

"No, I feel safe," I said. "It's okay. I think. What would happen if he just took off down the road at a full gallop?"

"Stop worrying," Molly said, and grinned again. "He's just trotting slowly. This is nothing, compared with how fast some pacers run around the track."

Little Brother was now moving at a good clip (or so I thought!). Sometimes he shook his head a little, and I could tell that he thought it was fun to pull the cart. The gravel road wound through the dark, quiet spruce woods. After a while we slowed to a walk, and Molly and I made small talk while Little Brother loped in front of the cart. Suddenly, Molly gave me the reins!

"Now it's your turn to drive," she said.

She showed me how to hold the reins and I took them, feeling only a little nervous. Little Brother seemed so far away, and I felt like if something happened, I couldn't really stop him!

"He's really strong," I said after a while. "He pulls on the bit the whole time."

"If you just move the reins a little, he'll be easier on the bit," Molly offered. "You should have soft but steady hands, exactly like you ride a horse. I think we should trot a little now before it gets too dark."

"But…" I tried to tell her it was a bad idea, but it was too late. Molly had already smacked Little Brother, who began to trot nicely with his powerful, long legs. All I could see were a large rear end and tail, and I prayed we wouldn't meet a car, or, even worse, a logging truck with a full load of logs. I managed to keep us on the road. Sometimes it felt as if we were dangerously close to the edge of the road, and a deep ditch was just waiting to swallow us all … But everything went well, to my huge relief, and as we walked into the stable yard I began to think trotting was really awesome!

We were just unhitching Little Brother when George appeared in the stable doorway. I decided not to let him bother me at all. Instead I concentrated completely on Little Brother.

"Where've you been?" George snarled. "I needed that new training cart an hour ago!"

"I asked my dad and he said I could take it," Molly said, trying to sound confident. "There's another cart."

"It has a flat tire," said George. "Your dad trusts me to do my job, but you're always getting in my way."

"Dad said that I could take the cart," Molly said, but with a little less confidence this time, which George noticed right away.

"He said you could take a little ride. You've been out for almost two hours!" he said with a sneer.

I kept my eyes on my job, looking closely at the straps that I was loosening. We hadn't been out as long as he said. I shot a look at the clock – we'd hardly been out for an hour, definitely no more than that. And George hadn't said a word to us before we left with the cart. He must have known that we were going to use it when we harnessed the horse!

"Okay, so – now you can have it," Molly said pulling the cart away from Little Brother.

"Look how dirty it is!" George sneered and pointed at it. "Make sure it's clean before you put it back in its place."

"Of course," Molly said. "I'll rinse it off later, after I take care of Little Brother."

"Do it now!" George said and his voice was hard and unpleasant.

"I can rinse it off," I said quietly to Molly. "Do you use the hose that's hanging by the stable door, or …?"

"No," Molly said. "Use the one on the other end. It's next to a cement platform which has a drain for the water."

I rolled the little cart out to the stable yard and pulled off by the place with the gravel drainage. It was so easy to clean – in fact there was hardly any dirt on it. I couldn't understand why George was complaining. All I found were some little bits of gravel and dust that had kicked up on it during our short trip.

I was almost finished when George rounded the corner. He examined the cart with a critical eye while I continued to let the water run over it. Suddenly he turned his gaze on me.

"Enough! That'll do," he said sharply, "or are you trying to take the paint off, too?"

"No, I wasn't," I answered calmly and turned off the water. My heart was pounding and I licked my lips nervously.

"I'm telling you once and for all that you're not welcome here," George said with a low voice. "We don't like snoops."

"I don't know what you're talking about!" I replied, trying to keep my voice steady. "I am not a snoop and Molly and I are friends. We go to school together."

George glared at me, and then gave me a half smile that never reached his eyes and was definitely not friendly.

"Why do you and Molly hang out here in the barn all the time, then? he asked.

"What?" I asked, buying myself a little time to think. "What're you talking about?"

"You know exactly what I'm talking about!" George said.

"Just lay off," I said, trying to sound tough – which was hard since I felt like a scared rabbit.

"Molly's my friend, and we're grooming her horse," I said, trying to sound calm and sure of myself. "It's obvious that we'd have to be in the stable, isn't it? And why shouldn't we be here?"

I heard how my voice sounded weak and not at all cocky like I wanted it to. And my words didn't make a very strong impression on George.

"This is a professional stable for pacer horses, not a riding school," George said. "I'm in charge. But how can I be when you two go around and take things without asking first – or play with the hay bales in the loft?"

"We weren't playing, I said. "We …"

I stopped talking when George leaned forward and stared me right in the eye.

"Watch out, Sara!" he threatened me. "Don't go snooping in my things, got that?"

Thankfully, at that second Molly rounded the corner and George straightened up.

"That'll be okay," he said in a pretend friendly voice. "Put it against the wall now."

I quickly pulled the cart over and set it down with the shafts upright.

"What happened?" Molly asked as soon as George was out of sight. "You're as white as a ghost."

"He threatened me!" I whispered in return, "But I don't want to talk about it now. We can talk later …"

Inside the barn, George had already begun to give the horses their evening meal. Neither Molly nor I wanted to be there a second more than we had to, so we hurried up to the main house. We got ourselves some sandwiches and iced tea, which we took upstairs to Molly's room.

"Okay, tell me now! What happened before I showed up?" Molly blurted out as soon as we'd sat down. She perched at the foot of her bed while I sat in the room's only armchair, which was worn-out, old and beige. I gripped my glass carefully while I told her what George had said to me.

When I was through, Molly was quiet for a moment.

She swirled her tea slowly even though the sugar must have dissolved a long time ago.

"He's up to something bad, that I'm sure of," she said at last.

"What do you think he could've hidden in the hayloft?" I wondered. "He really doesn't want us up there."

Molly nodded.

"The next time he and Dad go to the track, I'm going to go up there and look," she said decidedly. "But there's almost twelve tons of hay up there, and a whole lot more of straw, so it would be easy to hide something, and hard to find it – especially since I don't know exactly what I'm looking for …"

"You can at least say you're looking for the kittens if he catches you," I said, drinking my tea.

Molly laughed. "You must be crazy if you think I'm going up there when he's home!"

Chapter 4

The week flew by, and suddenly it was Friday again. Molly and I had discussed George's strange behavior quite a bit, both by phone and in school. In spite of George's threat, Molly had snuck up to the hayloft a couple of times and looked for whatever it was he was hiding.

"It's hopeless," she complained when we met at school on Friday. "I don't even know what I'm looking for! And there're a million neatly stacked hay bales. I can't move too many, or he'll know that someone's been up there."

I nodded.

"Maybe there's nothing there," I said as I took my math book from my locker. "Maybe he's always sour and disagreeable, and just wants us to stay away from him and the barn."

"Yeah, that's possible," Molly said with a sigh. "But one thing has come from all this – the mother cat has gotten used to me, and yesterday she let me scratch her head and back while she ate. And I think I know where she's hidden her kittens."

"How cool!" I said. "I hope she takes them to her food bowl soon."

"Me, too," Molly said. "Dad bought a whole carton of canned food, and I'm using it to entice her to come to me. It's the most deluxe cat food on the market – I'm sure she's never eaten this well in her whole life! Mom said that I should try to catch the kittens and take them into the heated saddle room. She's going to help me catch them when she has the time."

On Friday school ended early, and when I got home the house was quiet and empty. No one was there.

I got my book from my bedroom, and a snack in the kitchen, and then lay on the living room sofa, reading and listening to music.

I had almost finished two chapters when our black Labrador retriever, Swift, jumped up with a deafening bark and ran to the door. Mike walked into the house with Mom and Sophia, who had just come from town. Right behind them, Dad came in with two heavy bags of groceries.

Mike kicked off his sneakers and removed his jacket, and then he came into the living room while Swift circled around him with a well-chewed doggie toy in his mouth.

"Hi, sweetheart," he said, giving me a kiss. "How's it going?"

"Great," I said and felt the same way I always felt when I looked into Mike's sparkly blue eyes – totally warm inside. I like him so much!

"Finally, I'm finished with the job," Mike said, and sank into the armchair with obvious pleasure. "Now, as far as I can see, there's not much left to do on the barn! And

39

I told Hans that I wasn't going to lift a paintbrush again before Tuesday morning, at the earliest."

I smiled at Mike. I knew how tired he was, working so hard, and I knew he was really looking forward to finishing building the barn.

"What do you want to do tonight?" he asked, petting Swift on the head. Swift was wagging his black tail so hard that he almost knocked my cup off the coffee table.

"Suggestions?" Mike continued as I pushed Swift away.

"Nothing special … I thought about riding Winny on the trail for a while, and then maybe lunging Fandango. We trained for a long time yesterday and he doesn't need much work today," I said to Mike, who nodded.

Mike and I talked about the events of the previous week, and I told him all about what had happened at the Ridge Farm and about Molly's and my suspicions about George.

"That's awful," Mike said after I'd finished. "Maybe the guy feels responsible for how much hay the horses eat, or something like that. Stop worrying about it! It's not your problem he's so obnoxious."

"Agreed, but can't I at least wonder why?" I persisted. "Molly said that he's changed a whole lot in just a couple of months. She can hardly take care of her own horse any more."

"There might be other reasons," Mike said, absentmindedly scratching Swift behind his ears. "Maybe it's got nothing to do with the barn or the horses."

"Unlikely," I said shutting my book. "He's not about to threaten me over nothing. I've never done anything to him, ever!"

I sat up and put the book on the table.

"I hope Dad has dinner ready soon. I'm as hungry as a wolf! You're staying for dinner – right?"

Just then we heard angry voices coming from the kitchen, and I quietly sucked in my breath. Sophia was at it again. She's always in a bad mood, and she manages to pick a fight over nothing with Mom just about every day. But sometimes it's impossible to say who starts it – they're both hopeless!

"Alexandra and I are going to the dance tonight, and you can't stop me!" Sophia screamed. "We're going!"

"You're not going anywhere, young lady," Mom shouted, slamming her hand down. "You went out last weekend, and didn't come home until Sunday afternoon, even though I gave you money to take the evening bus home."

"I slept at Alexandra's," Sophia hissed. "What's the difference where I sleep – here or there?"

"There's a big difference!" Mom said. 'If we've agreed on one plan, then I expect you to follow through on what we agreed. And besides, how did you get to Alexandra's?"

"We … we took the bus!" Sophia said, but I could tell from her voice that she was lying.

"Really?" Mom said. "Alexandra's Mom called me at work today and said that you hitched a ride home because you'd missed the last bus. Two young girls hitching a ride in the middle of the night – don't you understand how dangerous that is?"

Sophia was silent.

"You were lucky to have been picked up by that old woman who drove you to Alexandra's. But that's the last time you do that – do you understand?"

Sophia still didn't answer.

"Gail and I have decided that you're both staying home tonight. And in the future you may not take the night bus home from town. Either Alexandra's parents or we will come and get you. Understood?"

"No way! Please, please, please," Sophia pleaded, "We won't miss the bus again, I promise. It was just …"

"No, you'll do as I say," Mom said forcefully, and I knew the discussion was over.

"This stinks! I never have any fun!" Sophia wailed, and came rushing out of the kitchen at top speed. She almost ran into Mike before turning and running up the stairs, taking them three at a time. She slammed her door with a terrific bang, and I looked at Mike with raised eyebrows.

"You were never like that, were you?" he said teasingly.

"Well," I said turning red. "It happened, but never as often as with Sophia."

And that was true. Sophia and I are very different – despite the fact that we're sisters and only two years apart in age.

Dad was in the kitchen making spaghetti sauce while Mom was setting the table. A huge bowl of steaming pasta was already on the table, and when I saw the mountain of shredded cheese on the plate beside the spaghetti, my mouth began to water.

"Can Mike eat over?" I asked, and Mom nodded.

"Sure," she said and put out another plate. "Sophia's probably going to stay up in her room and sulk for the rest of the evening, so there will be plenty of food."

We sat down and began to eat. Dad went up and knocked on Sophia's door and asked if she wanted to eat, but he only got an angry reply so he came down without her.

We ate in peace and quiet. Dad kept asking Mike questions about how Hans's new barn was coming. I felt embarrassed, but Mike knew how things were between Dad and Hans.

Dad and Hans had a major fight a few years ago, over some trees. The trees were on a hill and were ready to be cut down for logging, but Dad and Hans couldn't agree on which trees belonged to which farm. Finally they were forced to hire a guy to make up a map showing the boundary line between the two farms. Amazingly, it showed there was exactly the same number of trees on each side of the boundary line.

What's even sillier is that the trees are still standing on the hill today, even though the two men had settled who owned what years ago. Neither Dad nor Hans could make themselves chop them down, which is just as well as the trees are homes to mushrooms, which we pick every fall and use in cooking. The grudge has dragged on forever, though, and Dad and Hans haven't been friends for ages, but every now and then they're forced to see each other since Mike and I are friends. Neither Dad nor Hans was crazy about our friendship at the beginning – but they couldn't really object, either.

"I heard that you rode up to Ridge Farm last weekend, Sara," Dad said. "Which way did you go?"

"Past the gravel pit, and then we followed the road," I said, taking seconds on spaghetti. "It was long, but we galloped a lot, so the time actually flew by and didn't seem so bad."

"You do know about the path through the woods?" Dad

43

asked. "You know, the small path that goes away from the gravel pit … If you continue on it a ways, it turns into a real logging path. Then just follow it and you'll come out at the farm."

"I didn't know that," I said. "Strange, I've never ridden there."

Dad shrugged his shoulders.

"The road used to be very uneven, with big potholes, and there were so many better paths. And then the logging company put up a boom to stop the car traffic. It was difficult to get around the boom because there was so much stone and lumber. But we could go riding there someday and I'll show you the way –"

Just then a crash and a cry interrupted Dad's story.

"What's going on out there?" Dad shouted, and we all jumped up from the table and rushed out to the family room where the door opened up onto the patio.

On the lawn right next to the patio lay my little sister, moaning, one leg twisted under her at a weird angle. She whimpered softly. All around her were splintered bits of the wooden trellis that had been fastened to the house. It had obviously broken off from the wall when Sophia had tried to sneak out of the house by climbing out her bedroom window on the second floor.

"Sophia!" Mom yelled and rushed over to her as Sophia whined and tried to move a little.

"Lie still!" Dad said in a commanding voice. "Lie completely still! I'm going to call the ambulance. You could have a broken neck!"

He rushed into the house while Mike and I knelt carefully by Sophia. She looked at us and took a deep breath.

"It sure didn't hold my weight," she said in a weak voice. Mom quickly laid her hand on her shoulder to keep her from trying to get up.

"What were you thinking?" Mom said in a voice more anxious than angry. "Were you climbing down on the trellis?"

"My bad, my bad … I just wanted to go to the dance," Sophia said with tears streaming down her face. "I just had to go … so I thought I'd climb down, and then …"

She began to cry with long, shaky sobs, and I felt a sob rising in my own throat. I couldn't bear to think about her being hurt – it was too awful. She might even be crippled for life. Just think, if she could never walk, ride a bike or run! It was too horrible.

I felt my own tears stinging my eyes, and Mike quietly put his arm around my shoulders and hugged me hard.

"My leg," sobbed Sophia. "It hurts …"

"Can you feel your leg?" Mom asked seriously, and Sophia nodded.

"Yeah … it hurts so much … ohhh …"

Her face was pale, and she suddenly turned her head to the left and threw up. To keep from watching her I turned away and looked up at her open window, with its white curtain hanging out and a flowerpot sitting on the edge. It wasn't that far from the ground, since our house isn't very tall, but Sophia landed the wrong way.

"It's a good sign that you can feel the pain in your leg, Sophia," Mom said calmly. "That means you haven't broken your back, at least. Just lie still. Can you move your hands? Fingers? Can you feel your whole body?"

Sophia carefully moved her fingers just as Dad arrived

with a damp cloth. He wiped her mouth and spread an old newspaper over her vomit.

At that same moment we heard a throbbing motor, and over the treetops we could see a little spot coming toward our farm. It was the medivac helicopter.

"Quickly, get the horses in!" Dad yelled to me. Mike and I ran out to the pasture. Winny was already upset by the strange sound, and when I grabbed her halter and tried to lead her to the barn she pranced excitedly. I thought she was going to pull my arm out of its socket, and I breathed a sigh of relief when she went right into her stall.

Mike was right behind us with Camigo and Fandango, while old Maverick just ran into his stall by himself.

We had just finished getting the horses in when the helicopter landed in the clearing at the other side of the driveway across from our farm. The huge rotor blades whirled around while the machine slowly lowered to the ground. The blades created a wind that made the grass lie down flat, and I was sure that if we hadn't gotten the horses inside, all four would have run away into the woods! Then I got mad at myself. How could I think about the horses when Sophia was lying on the ground, seriously injured?

A doctor, a nurse, two EMTs and the pilot all piled out of the chopper. The doctor began to examine Sophia, who was now lying completely still. I listened to him talk to her, and she mumbled and whimpered her answers. I felt the lump in my throat grow – If only she wouldn't – It can't be too bad! It just can't!

I couldn't see exactly what they did because Mike and I were standing off to the side, but they soon put her on a stretcher and the EMTs carried her to the helicopter. She wore a thick neck brace to help keep her head completely still, and I swallowed and swallowed to try to keep the lump in my throat from turning into sobs …

Mom went in the helicopter to the hospital while Dad ran to get the car to drive there. When the helicopter's huge rotor blades started up I couldn't hold back the tears any longer, and I began to cry as it lifted up into the sky. Mike put his arm around me and hugged me hard while I just cried and said nothing.

Just as the helicopter flew off, Mike started to laugh.

"What is it?" I said, and looked at him through teary eyes. "Why are you laughing?"

"Your sister's not too smart," Mike said calmly, hugging me even harder. "She should have milked it a little longer. You know what? I saw her wave to us from the window! She'll be okay!"

Chapter 5

The cheerful yellow and white corridors of the hospital were as welcoming as possible. On the walls were small colorful paintings with nature scenes, and through the open doors of different rooms we could see patients lying down or sitting up in their beds while visitors sat or stood and talked with them.

Mike and I had driven into town to say hello to Sophia during hospital visiting hours. I could see from the magazine pile on Sophia's bedside table that Mom and Dad had been there earlier. They must have stopped at every newsstand and cleaned them out of all the weekly magazines they could find.

"Hi," said Sophia cheerfully. She seemed incredibly lively and fresh looking, and was lying in bed skimming through the latest fashion magazine.

"Hi, how's it going?" I said, pulling a chair over to her bedside.

"Not too bad," Sophia said, frowning. "It was bad last night when they were screwing my leg together, but it feels better now. They say that I can go home in a few days."

"That's great news," Mike said, and gave Sophia the book – a love story from the series *Love at the Hospital* that we'd brought with us. I knew Sophia would enjoy it.

"Nowadays, you don't have to stay in the hospital long with a broken leg," Sophia said, as if she knew everything about hospitals and broken legs. "I don't have a plaster cast either. My leg is held together with steel screws. It's so much simpler and better than the old days!" she continued, and threw off the covers so we could see what it looked like.

"But you'll have to have crutches, won't you?" I asked, and Sophia nodded.

"Of course."

"Now you've got to tell us why you were climbing out the window," I said. "How could you ever think that little dinky trellis would hold you?"

Sophia blushed and actually looked a little embarrassed.

"Well, I just thought that … that it'd hold. Then when I felt it start to come away from the wall, I tried to climb in again, but I lost my grip, and so … the rest you know. I fell and landed wrong!"

Just then we heard voices from the corridor. Alexandra, her brother and a pair of guys in the group my sister usually hangs out with walked in. They had flowers and chocolates with them, and everyone talked at once, so after a couple of minutes Mike and I felt like we were in the way.

We said good-bye and left when Sophia started to retell the story of what happened, including a bunch of new details that she'd left out when she told us the same story right before they arrived.

It was sprinkling out when we left to drive down to the center of town. We decided to go to the library and then get some hot chocolate or tea at a small café. I was so glad that we were doing something together. Mike held my hand as we ambled along the sidewalks. Most of the tiny shops were already closed as it was Sunday afternoon, but the library was open, and it was bright and welcoming after the rain.

The back of the library has a brand new computer room and Mike, who doesn't have a home computer since lightning destroyed his during the last thunderstorm, went to check his e-mail. I went with him, and no sooner had I entered the room than I saw someone I knew – George!

He was sitting at a computer station in the corner, concentrating on the screen. It seemed like he had a hard time seeing, because he was learning forward and peering with wide eyes. Suddenly he looked up, and when he saw me his expression changed from surprise to irritation. I knew that he recognized me, but he didn't make any effort to say hello, so I didn't either.

He got up quickly and left the room, heading toward the small café in a corner of the library.

Curious, I went over to the computer where he'd been sitting and looked at the screen. It was blank. He'd apparently logged off before he jumped up and left.

I looked around to make sure he was truly gone, and then logged back onto the Internet.

"What're you doing?" Mike asked with interest from his own machine.

"Well, I thought I'd check my e-mail while I wait for you," I said.

"Okay," Mike said. "But I'm finished. I'll go and browse through the mystery section for a while."

When he left I was alone in the room. I checked the browser to see which sites the weird horse caretaker had been visiting. It really didn't matter to me – it was just simply my uncontrollable curiosity!

Suddenly I noticed a movement by the door, and when I looked over, the nasty George was standing there again! He glared at me and I felt my panic grow. Why was he standing there glaring at me? I'd never done anything to bother him. It was just then that the page he'd been on last came up on the screen!

Oh, what a bummer! I was sure that he knew I was spying on him, and my cheeks reddened and got burning hot. Embarrassed, I clicked out of the site and went to a horse site I like. George stayed in the doorway, his arms crossed. It seemed that he was guarding me, to keep me from leaving, and I swallowed a big gulp. Oh, no! Would he ever leave? And where was Mike? I wished he would come back right away.

I pretended that nothing was wrong and bent near the screen to read an article about hoof rot.

"What're you doing?"

Mike's voice startled me, and I breathed easy as I saw him pass by the man in the doorway.

"I found an interesting article on how to care for a horse with hoof rot," I said with a smile. "You ought to read it!"

Mike looked at the screen.

"I subscribe to that magazine," he said, shrugging his shoulders. "You can borrow it from me instead of sitting here and reading. C'mon, let's go eat. I'm hungry!"

The café was almost empty, and we sat by the corner window. We each ordered hot chocolate with milk and a sub with ham, cheese, lettuce, tomatoes, onions, pickles and black olives.

While waiting for the food to arrive I told him about George and why I was sitting at that particular computer. Mike gave me a teasing grin and shook his head.

"You're hopelessly curious," he said, and put his hand over mine. "Okay, what page was he looking at? A harness racing page?"

"No, actually not," I said. "I didn't have time to see much – but I do remember what the title was – Prescription Drugs."

"Prescription Drugs?" Mike said with surprise. "What does that mean?"

"I don't know," I said, confused. "There was a picture of a huge pill jar with lots of loose pills around it and the words 'Prescription Drugs' written over it. I didn't have time to look any more because he showed up again. He looked really mad, and I felt like the creep was watching me. I was glad that you came back so quickly."

Mike shrugged his shoulders.

"Maybe he just wanted that particular computer, so he was waiting until you were done?" Mike said, and then added, " I thought he looked like an ordinary guy who was just standing around waiting for something. I think you let your imagination run away with you."

Mike wasn't taking me seriously, so I dropped the subject. I decided, however, to log onto that site when I got home. I wanted to have a look at it where I was safe and wouldn't be disturbed. Maybe I was nosy about some things, but … if it hadn't been for George's strange behavior at Molly's I wouldn't have gotten interested in the first place, I thought as I took another swallow of my now cool chocolate.

When we got home it was still gray and cloudy, but the rain had stopped, so Mike suggested we work with Winny on jumping. He offered to set up and build all the obstacles, and I happily accepted his help.

Dad is usually the one who puts up everything and then tries to give me all his good advice. I just get so … so frustrated! I know they mean well, but moms and dads shouldn't try to teach their children – it just doesn't work!

Dad was a champion field jumper at one time, but that was practically back in the Stone Age. Since then, he hardly even walks his horse in the woods; Mom's the one who trots away on old Maverick. Dad would rather play soccer or computer games.

Dad used to work as a contractor, but not any more. He and his friend Ben started a computer business a few years ago. Dad and Ben had big plans, and even though Mom was nervous about his being able to support us, Dad was really happy to leave contracting.

I rushed up to my room to change while Mike drove home to do the same. After getting my riding pants and sweatshirt on, I realized that I still had some free time before Mike got back, so I turned on the computer and logged onto the Internet. We just got high-speed broadband Internet access at home, and it's great not having to wait all the time for pages to load.

I began my search and quickly found George's page again. It had a dark background and a picture of a pill container with the top off. Around the container were lots of pills spread out, and in white luminescent letters half a word, "pres…" Curious, I clicked down the page to see what this was, but I wasn't allowed to go too far down. I would have to register as a user in order to go further, but I understood that this was a place to buy prescription drugs over the Internet. I had heard about this before and I also knew some of the sites were illegal.

Deep in thought, I turned off the computer, wondering why a horse caretaker would have an interest in that page. And why would he look at that page in a public library? Almost everyone has a computer at home. Maybe his computer got fried in the last thunderstorm – just like Mike's?

I got up and hurried out to the stable. I could tell that Mom had already ridden because Maverick was in his stall eating hay. I brought Winny in from the pasture, and while I was brushing her I decided to stop thinking about that web page. I would probably never know the answer, so I just let the brush slide over Winny's chestnut brown coat. That obnoxious George had the right to look at whatever sites he wanted. But even though I promised to let it go, a thought still gnawed at me …

Finally I had Winny saddled and bridled, and I tried to concentrate on her instead. Her coat gleamed, her eyes were shining bright with the anticipation of a ride, and I stroked her neck happily. Mom and Dad weren't sure Winny was the right horse for me when I first got her, but now both of them really love her. Dad even rides her sometimes, and a couple of times I even caught him muttering jealously that he would have loved having a great horse like Winny back in his competition riding days.

Winny's only fault is that she's lively and intelligent, and sometimes she can be very difficult to ride because she has such a strong will of her own. More than once I've wondered whether I'm in over my head with her. But at the same time, deep down, I know that Winny is the best horse in the world for me. When we have a huge task ahead of us, I know that Winny's the best horse for the job.

I led her out to the stable yard and mounted her. Mike hadn't come back yet, so we walked around the track with long reins, and then after a while I led her into a trot. Winny felt tense and energetic, but after a couple of rounds she calmed down. She pulled at the bit, lowered her head and began to work with her whole body. I looked at my watch and saw that Mike was late. Strange, I thought. He was only going home to change clothes. But just then, Mike came roaring into the driveway in his little white car. He stopped on a dime so the wheels left long imprints on the gravel, hopped out and slammed the door hard.

"What's wrong?" I asked as I rode over to the fence. I was worried – Mike's never like this. "Did something happen?"

"I'm furious," Mike hissed. "I am so fed up with Hans and his demands that I gave him my notice. I'm quitting."

"What?" I broke in, "Quitting? But ..."

"I'm sorry, Sara," Mike said and looked me in the eye. "I know it means I might have to move away from here, but I've done enough work for that slave driver!"

Chapter 6

I sat completely still and stared at Mike without knowing what to say. He looked furious, and when he began to tell me in a low voice what had happened I knew that his fury was justified.

"You know how much I've worked the past few months, right?" he asked, and I nodded and patted Winny on the neck.

Hans and Maggie's barn had burned down at the beginning of the summer, and Mike and Hans had worked long and hard to rebuild it. It was finished now – a beautiful new stable with large stalls, bright colors and all the modern conveniences, including a fancy new watering system.

"Hans promised me that I could have this whole weekend and the beginning of next week off to catch up on my own life. Just now, when I went over, he asked me to build a new fence for the stallion pasture. I was hardly out of the car before he started demanding that I come and help him! I said that he'd promised me time off, and then he said that if I didn't pitch in right then when I was needed that I could find another job."

"And?" I whispered, too anxious to speak louder.

"I told him I quit," Mike said, shrugged his shoulders and came onto the riding track.

"But where'll you go?" I asked. "What will you do for a job? And …"

"I don't know!" Mike said, and began to bang the obstacles together. "But it'll all come together. I'm sure of it!"

I watched a determined and hard-working Mike build the jumps for me, and felt a sob sit like a lump in my throat. If Mike didn't work for Hans and Maggie, he would have to move away. And if he moved – then I would lose him! Dear Mike … I was stunned!

"Will you move?" I asked and swallowed my lump. "Where will you go, if you have to move?"

"I don't know," said Mike and he gave me a look. "Well, I'm studying in town this semester, so I'll definitely stay in the area, at least until Christmas."

"And where would you live then?" I asked.

"It'll work out," Mike said.

"But …" I began again, but Mike put up his hand for me to stop asking, so I stopped.

"It only happened ten minutes ago, Sara. Right now I have no ideas about anything! Do you want to jump, or shall we just call it a day? I'm willing to help you, only if you want help, but I have no desire to discuss my future any further. Okay?"

I looked at him and felt the tears burn my eyes. I blinked a couple of times, shortened Winny's reins and sucked in my breath.

"We'll jump," I said quietly. "What're you going to build for jumps?"

"A row of cavalettis in the middle, and then a little jump on the right and one on the left. You should trot over the cavalettis and then swing in a different direction after each. I want you to stay focused and steady so you can regulate the speed and steer her where you want her to go."

I nodded and began to trot. All my happiness was gone with the wind, although I still tried to concentrate on my riding and couldn't help but smile at Winny's free spirit. She shook her head energetically, and I was glad that I remembered to put her martingale on or she would have knocked my nose with her head. She kept her head low so I could barely hold her, and even when Mike raised both oxers and the upright jump to about 45 inches she flew over them like a bird. It was difficult at first for her to trot calmly over the cavaletti booms and then turn to the right or left and make a jump. She ran over the cavalettis the first few times in a gallop so they went in every direction, and I was afraid that we'd crash! When she was finally able to do it the way I wanted we called it quits.

Winny gets excited easily, and then she gets sloppy when she's tired, so I have be sensitive to her needs and quit before that happens.

I had just slowed her to a walk and relaxed the reins when Winny suddenly stopped in her tracks, raised her head and stared at the road. I patted her calmly on the neck – and turned to see Molly and Little Brother coming down the road. Winny whinnied happily at Little Brother and began to dance in place. I pushed her forward and she began to do a strange halting walk, lifting her legs high and keeping her neck straight – trying to impress the little brown Standardbred who was so good as to come calling on her!

I stopped Winny at the fence and Mike came over to us.

"Hi!" I said to Molly. "How did you find us?" I introduced the two of them.

"My Dad showed me on a map, so it wasn't hard," Molly said while Little Brother pulled his head down and began to graze. "This is an awesome riding track," she continued.

"Thanks, I like it, although it's a little too small and the jumps aren't as great as they should be."

"That's nothing," Molly said. "The most important thing is that you have obstacles to jump over! I've nagged my dad to at least fix a pair of hurdles for me, but he never has time."

"You can use the jumps here if you want," I suggested and waved toward the obstacles. "I'm the only one who uses the course. You're welcome to use it any time!"

"Are you sure?" Molly blushed as she asked. "What if I broke something, or … we're not so great, Little Brother and I … and you're in training. We'd only be in your way."

"No, it's okay," I said. "Mount up and give it a try. I've already finished."

I dismounted from Winny and took her into the stable. She was damp with sweat and I sponged her off and put a heavy sweat blanket on her, then I put her in her stall and gave her some hay.

I went back to the track where Mike was helping Molly train Little Brother to jump. Even from a distance I could see that it wasn't going very well. Little Brother almost always hit the cavalettis and he often came at the obstacle completely wrong so that Molly had to jerk him in the mouth or hit his flank – or both.

Finally Molly pulled Little Brother to a stop and sighed deeply. I could hear how disappointed she was.

"He can't and I can't," she said sorrowfully. "Together we're really horrible. Maybe it's best if we don't do it."

"Have you done much jumping before?" I asked, and Molly shook her head.

"I've ridden mostly for fun in the woods. When I was younger I had a Gotland horse that I rode and used to pull a cart, but he got a bad case of laminitis and we had to have him put down. Dad didn't have enough money to buy me a new pony, so I got Little Brother instead, mostly because no one else wanted him."

She dismounted and loosened the saddle girth and Little Brother lowered his head at once and began to graze as if he'd never seen green grass before.

I felt so sorry for Molly. She seemed to have ambition and did what she could, but Little Brother wasn't the best horse to learn how to jump with. He was a beginner too, and needed to have an experienced rider who could guide him the right way.

Suddenly I had a brilliant idea!

"If you want, you can borrow my pony and train with him. He's gentle and well broken-in," I said to Molly who looked surprised.

"Do you mean …? I couldn't handle Fandango. He's clever, but way too much for me."

"I didn't mean Fandango," I said. "I also have a pony named Camigo. He's only 13.2 hands, but you're small and he's easy to ride."

"Well …" Molly said doubtfully. "But …"

"No buts!" I said. "I'll go get him so you can try him out."

I ran to the pasture behind the barn and got Camigo. I brought him inside, fastened him with crossties and quickly brushed him, put on his saddle and bridle and whispered in his ear that he should be extra nice and well behaved.

As I was leading him out to Molly I couldn't help but think that it was sheer luck that I had ridden him now and then during the last month. He wasn't in the best shape, but he should certainly be able to leap over the low jumps with no problem. And besides – most important of all – he would think this was great fun!

I took hold of Little Brother's reins while Molly, who was still clearly doubtful, got up in the saddle and adjusted the stirrup length. Camigo snorted when he saw the jumps and walked quickly into the ring with light steps and a happy gleam in his eyes. I smiled when I saw him. Camigo is a terrific pony, and we'd won oodles of ribbons together not too long ago.

I stood by the fence and held Little Brother, who kept grazing like a starved horse. Mike gave Molly some good tips and advice on how to sit in the saddle and hold the reins, and then she put Camigo through a walk, trot and canter.

I leaned against the fence and tried to concentrate on Mike helping Molly, but I couldn't help it – his earlier announcement kept buzzing in my head.

I tried to remember what life was like before Mike … what did I do with my time? Hung out in the stable, rode my horse, read lots of books. Hung around with my friend

Jessie too, but now that she's moved to England we can only e-mail each other.

I felt a lump in my throat, and I had to bite my lower lip to keep from sobbing.

That darned Hans! Why is he so unpleasant all the time? Mike worked his tail off all summer, and he deserves a few days off. Oh, how I hate Hans, that old geezer.

I swallowed and swallowed again, blinking away the tears as I tried to concentrate on the horse and rider in the ring. Mike kept the cavalettis but rebuilt the obstacles to simple crosses instead. Camigo lifted his feet too high over the cavaletti poles and then flew over the cross jump with a look that said, "Watch me – aren't I the world's best?!" I couldn't help but smile at his expression. He's so wonderful, my little Camigo!

Mike and I worked together to build a slightly higher jump for Molly. First we built a little cross, then two gallop steps and then an oxer. The first little cross jump was a guide for Camigo so he would be in rhythm for the oxer, since Molly didn't really know the routine.

Camigo raised his head, and I could see his happiness when he galloped at full speed toward the jump. Molly kept a light seat, leaned forward and together they succeeded in jumping the two obstacles as if they were nothing! Mike raised the bar on the oxer a little bit more so it was about thirty inches high, and Camigo flew over it as Molly smiled with joy.

"That's good," Mike called out, and Molly reined in Camigo who didn't want to stop. He snorted and threw his head, and I knew he wanted to jump just one more time and then one more time …

Molly walked him over to me and I saw how happy she was.

"That was awesome! The most fantastic ride I've ever had!" she said enthusiastically, patting Camigo on the neck. "What a wonderful horse! I've never jumped this high before. Never! I can't believe I dared …"

I grinned at Molly.

"You can borrow him anytime," I said. "He just hangs out here in the pasture and does nothing but graze for most of the day."

Molly stared at me with her mouth hanging open.

"Do you really mean that?" she said at last and stroked Camigo's mane. "Are you sure?"

"I promise, it's for real!" I said and couldn't help laughing. "I'll ask my parents, but I'm sure they won't mind. Why don't you cool him off now, and I'll take him in later."

Molly nodded and began to walk around the ring with long reins. Little Brother watched her with a melancholy look and a large wad of unchewed grass hanging from his mouth.

"I think you have a competitor, old man," I said in a friendly voice as I patted him on the neck. "But pay attention, because your mistress will learn a lot from Camigo – and then she'll teach you."

Molly walked Camigo for a while, then dismounted and took care of Little Brother. It wasn't yet late, but if she wanted to get home before dark she'd have to leave right away.

Mike and I waved as she headed toward the gravel road, and then Mike put his arm around my shoulders.

"That was nice of you to let her ride Camigo," he said.

I smiled and felt a warm feeling for being generous.

"You know Camigo loves to jump, so it was just as much for his sake as for hers," I said.

We led Camigo into the stable and I started to unsaddle him. Mike helped me, and neither of us said much while we brought the other two horses in and gave them all their evening meal.

It was time to turn on the stable lights. As I did so, I watched Mike quietly standing in the doorway. He stood out like a black silhouette against the still-light night sky.

"What're you thinking about?" I asked as I went to him, feeling the tears burn in my eyes.

"What can I do now?" he mumbled quietly.

"I don't want you to move!" I said and couldn't stifle the sob. "I won't let you!"

Mike put both hands on my face and looked deep into my eyes.

"I don't want to move, Sara. I promise I'll do all I can to stay here. But I have to have a job to support myself. You know that …"

I nodded quietly, but I couldn't help the pain inside.

Chapter 7

I couldn't think about anything except Mike and Hans's fight during the next few days.

Mike was at our house almost the whole time since he didn't like being alone in his little cottage, just a stone's throw from Hans and Maggie's house.

Maggie came by one evening and spoke with Mike, but they didn't get anywhere. After she left, Mike told me what they had discussed. The gist of it was that Hans was furious with Mike for quitting. Maggie was asking Mike to come back to work. Maggie is really nice, and she's also one of my Mom's best friends, but even her friendly manner and words weren't enough for Mike. He'd made up his mind, and there was no going back. That was clear!

What Mike wanted to do, however, was anything but clear. In the past few months he had often said that he was so tired he just wanted to quit. But now he kept hinting that maybe, just *maybe* he would go and have a talk with Hans. After all, there were a lot of advantages to the job …

The only person pleased with the situation was Dad, who went around looking like the cat that had swallowed the canary. He never said it straight out, but you just knew he wanted to tell Mike, "*what did I tell you about Hans, and now you know I was right?!*" Both Mike and I tried to avoid him as much as possible.

I told Molly what happened and she tried to cheer me up – but there wasn't much to be cheerful about. One moment I could understand Mike's point of view exactly and agree that now that poor Hans had to do all the work it served him right. And the next moment, anxiety crept into my thoughts: how would Mike manage to support himself without a job? Where would he live? If he moved away – so far away that we couldn't keep seeing each other, what would happen to us as a couple?

When I came home from school on Tuesday it was raining. Tuesday was my late day at school, which meant that I had to take the last school bus home. It was almost 4:30 when I stepped off the bus at my stop, and my back-pack was heavy with all the schoolbooks that I'd packed for homework. I knew I had lots of homework, and I wasn't looking forward to doing it. How I hated Tuesdays!

I had just changed into my horse clothes and made a sandwich when a car drove into the yard. Sophia entered the kitchen on crutches, smiling a slanted little suffering smile.

"Well," I said, "how's the leg?"

"Completely fine," Sophia said and panted a little over the extra work it took to hop with crutches. "Hey, will you make me one of those cheese sandwiches with a pickle? Please?"

"Well, hello," mom protested. "We're going to eat soon! You shouldn't have a snack so close to dinner."

"I haven't eaten anything since my lunch at school," I whined, getting up. "I'll starve if I don't get something in my stomach before I take care of the horses!"

Mom muttered something while Sophia laid her head on the table.

"Please, won't you make me one of those sandwiches? I can't stand up very well, and …"

"No," I said and went to the door. "I'm in a hurry. I need to ride before it gets pitch dark."

"Be kind now, Sara!" Dad said as he came into the kitchen and heard Sophia.

"No," I said. "Help her yourself."

"Boy, aren't you crabby!" Sophia shot back in a disagreeable voice, and her good mood flew away with the wind. "That's the thanks I get for letting your friend ride my pony!"

"*Your* pony?" I said, raising my eyebrows in shock. "When's the last time you took care of him, if I may ask? I'll loan him out to anyone I want. It was courteous of me to tell you that I'd done it in the first place."

"Sometimes I take care of Camigo!" Sophia hissed. "I rode him quite a bit this summer."

"Really? I said, raising my eyebrows. "When?"

"You know that I rode him!" Sophia said, and I knew that I had no energy to spare arguing with her.

"And besides …" she continued, but I didn't hear the rest of it as I was already out the door. My stable shoes were on the porch, and while I was knotting the shoestrings I was thinking how nice it would be in the stable, mucking out the stalls in peace and quiet. After being with a million people at school all day, then arguing with Sophia and getting criticized by Mom and Dad, there was nothing more wonderful than going out to the predictably quiet, calm stable and cleaning up after the horses.

But the stable was clean and neat, with new straw in all the stalls and hay in the bins. I guessed that Mike had been there, and I was whistling happily when I went out to get the horses.

But to my surprise, Winny was missing! Fandango, Camigo and Maverick all stood at the gate and waited like they always did – but Winny wasn't with them.

I went into the pasture and called for her, but I didn't see her anywhere! I was ice cold with fear – what if she'd gotten out? I've seen her jump over the fence – she did it the day she arrived at our farm. She'd been afraid of Camigo, and after tearing around the pasture a few times at a full gallop, she flew over the fence like a bird. Later she ran around Hans's newly plowed fields before I succeeded in capturing her with a grain bucket.

But that was a long time ago – and now she was very happy with the three guy horses. I didn't think she would have run away on her own. At least I was pretty sure, and when I checked all the electric fences they were fine.

Just then I heard hooves and I turned around. Winny came trotting from the lower pasture with her head and tail held on high alert. She was full of energy and seemed happy, and I was so relieved to see my beautiful brown horse.

"Hi, Winny! It's time to go in," I said softly as I tried to take hold of her halter. But she wouldn't let me near her.

She pranced around with a playful look in her eyes, and I smiled at her mischief. She was so beautiful!

I started to take Fandango, Camigo and Maverick in instead. After all three had gone in, Winny stood at the gate and nibbled on it nervously, which is exactly what I hoped she would do. She doesn't like to be in the pasture by herself.

I caught her, and when I fastened the lead rope to her halter I gave her a few pellets as a reward for standing still and letting me catch her.

After all four horses had their hay and were chewing contentedly, I went up to the house. It was almost supper-time, and I was so hungry I could eat – well, almost anything. After dinner I wanted to ride both Fandango and Winny in our little ring.

Josie the instructor's comment about dressage training had at least given me a little bit of a bad conscience – I really ought to train more dressage with Fandango. He's very large and strong for a pony, and if he decides not to mind me, I can't guide him. If he's in perfect shape, we should have a chance of placing in the fall horse shows.

When I went back to the kitchen I saw the mail lying on the sideboard, and I wouldn't have thought anything of it, but Mom took an envelope and handed it to me.

"Here, Sara, you have a letter."

Somewhat surprised, I took the envelope and examined it. "What's this? I'm not expecting any mail."

It was an ordinary white envelope with no return address. My name and address weren't even handwritten. They looked as if they were printed on a label by a computer. Maybe it's an advertisement for something, I thought.

I opened the envelope and unfolded the letter. It was a normal white sheet of paper, and in the middle was one sentence, "Watch out, Sara!"

I just stared at the three words as my heart started to race. Was this a joke?

"Hey, what is it?" Sophia said, curious. "You look as if you've seen a ghost!"

"Look at this strange letter," I said, and held it so both Mom and Sophia could see what was written.

"What now?" Mom said, raising an eyebrow. "A threatening letter? What have you gotten yourself into now, Sara?"

"Nothing!" I answered honestly. "I have no idea what it means, I swear!"

At that moment, Mike appeared in the hallway and walked into the kitchen with a huge smile.

"Hi all," he greeted us happily. He looked at the paper I held in my hand and raised his eyebrows.

"What's this?" he asked. "Did something happen?"

"Sara got a letter," Sophia said. "Read it and you'll see. It's a threatening letter!"

I gave him the envelope and he looked at it as carefully as I had just done.

"Suspicious," he said, and handed me the paper and envelope again. "Do you have any idea what this is about?"

"Not a clue!" I said. "Do you think Hans could be behind it? Maybe he thinks I influenced you to quit?"

Mike looked at me thoughtfully, and then shook his head emphatically.

"No, he would never do anything like that. Sure, he's

furious, but he's more of the screaming and fighting type. He's a decent guy, even if he is a slave driver."

I nodded. I don't like Hans and how he behaves, but I knew Mike was right.

"All that aside, Hans and I haven't spoken to each other today," Mike said as he put his arm on my shoulders. "I've decided – I really am quitting work."

I felt my anxiety take hold of me, and suddenly the letter no longer seemed important.

"That's just awful," I said, sucking in my breath. "Then … then you'll be moving after all?"

"Yeah, but not for a little while," Mike said. "I'm going to stay and work there for about another month. I'll quit when I've found something new."

"Okay," I said and drew in my breath. A month would buy us some time … but then Mike might move away for good – and what would happen to us? I didn't dare think about it.

"You can try to get another job around here, Mike," Mom said, understanding my sadness.

"Yeah, there's going to be a job opening for a horse caregiver at the riding school. We'll see," Mike said. I swallowed and inside I prayed silently to myself, *please, let him get the job … let him get the job … please, please…*

Just then, Dad appeared and I tried to push aside all thoughts of Mike's eventual move as best I could. Naturally Dad saw the letter and he was just as curious as we had been before.

"Do you have any idea who wrote this – or why?" he asked, scratching his head.

"No!" I said. "I don't have any enemies, I haven't

71

heard or seen anything strange, and I haven't been spying on anyone…"

"Wait a minute, you have," Mike interrupted. "What about Molly's dad's sourpuss horse trainer – George!"

"Oh, yeah," I said. "It …"

"What?" Mom quizzed me. "Who's the sourpuss horse trainer?"

I told them all what had happened and Mom sighed.

"It sounds really far-fetched," Mom said. "But one never knows, of course. The world's full of crazy people."

"What should I do now?" I said, sighing deeply. "Call the police?"

"It's going a little too far to call them this late at night, but I think you should call them tomorrow and let them know," Dad said and gave me the letter and the envelope. "Why not go to Andrew Roos tomorrow and tell him everything and see what he says?"

Andrew Roos is one of the young policemen at the station, and we'd been in touch with him several times during the summer – for example, when we saved those horses that were dying from lack of water and food. He's easy to talk to, and I knew I could trust him a hundred percent.

I nodded, folded the letter and stuffed it in the envelope. It was finally time to eat. I had been starving before, but now my stomach was in such a hard knot of anxiety that the food almost made me nauseated.

And Sophia's teasing didn't make things any better.

"Just think, Sara," she said in a sarcastic tone. "You're getting to be like those private detectives I see on TV. Exciting things are always happening to you!"

72

I glared daggers at Sophia. More than enough quirky things had happened this summer, and I didn't have the slightest desire to become a private detective.

"You have my permission to take over as the family detective," I said, irritated. "It's not a role I chose for myself!"

"Maybe!" Sophia said snottily, and then she quickly changed the topic.

After dinner I went out to the stable to take care of Fandango. Although I tried to think about other things the letter and its meaning just swirled around in my head. It made me more nervous than I cared to admit, and George's angry face, piercing eyes and threatening voice kept appearing in my head.

Being unpleasant is no crime, I thought to myself as I tried time and again to forget the whole thing. But deep inside, I was already convinced that it was George who sent the letter. Who else could it have been? There was no one else!

Chapter 8

The next day I met Molly in the cafeteria. We had the same lunch period and tried to eat lunch together as often as possible. We sat down at a corner table and I showed her the letter and told her what had happened. Molly didn't say anything, but although she tried to hide her feelings, I could tell she was upset.

"What's the matter?" I asked.

"Sunday night when I was brushing Little Brother and Dad had just gone in, George came out to the stable. He wasn't his usual nasty self – he chatted, quite friendly with me, which surprised me. Then after a while he asked me what your last name was.

"Really," I said and folded the paper and put it away again. "Did he say why he wanted to know?"

"No ... but boy, do I have a bad conscience, Sara. I shouldn't have told him, but I didn't know how I could not say without causing a problem ... Are you mad at me?"

"No, of course not," I said calmly. "It's not exactly a

74

secret – and besides, it just makes me more sure that he's the one who sent the letter to me."

"Yes," Molly said, and then she continued, "You remember our search for the mother cat and her kittens? They're in the warm saddle room right now. Someone found them and moved them there!"

"Your mom or dad?" I asked, but Molly shook her head

"No, George! Believe it or not … He made a nice bed in a box and put out food and water for them. He's so strange sometimes. He can be as nasty as can be toward people – but he's always kind to animals."

"Yeah, and now we have no excuse to go looking around the hayloft," I said and flashed a crooked smile at Molly. "Smart, real smart!"

"You're right," Molly said, putting her hand over her mouth. "Why didn't I think of that?!"

"Have you told your parents how nasty he is to us when we're in the barn?" I asked, and Molly nodded.

"Yeah, but Dad just says we should pay no attention to him. George is a magician with horses, and it's not easy to find someone that good who's willing to work way out in the country."

"Where'd he work before?" I asked.

"With a professional trainer who was working with Black Babe," Molly said. "When we moved here, we brought Black Babe home with us, and George followed as her manager and trainer. Or actually – Dad offered him the job and he took it. Unfortunately! Oh, I've got to split – I've got chemistry in five minutes!"

Molly got up, took her lunch tray and headed toward the exit. I just sat there and let my thoughts run free. It seemed obvious that George was the one who sent the letter to me. It wasn't as if there was anyone else to suspect.

After school I went to the police station and asked the clerk if I could talk with Andrew Roos. Unfortunately he was on vacation, but there was another policeman that I could talk with, so I headed toward a room at the end of the corridor.

The policeman that I talked to was named Art, and I can't remember his last name. He tried his best to make me feel like a child playing detective. Of course, he did take notes – at least he scribbled on his notepad – but from the start I knew that he thought I was silly to have come in with my letter.

"It's probably one of your buddies playing a joke on you," he said with a dismissive puff when I had finished speaking.

It was hot in the room. Art was a huge muscular man. The hair on the top of his head was thin and white and he had a well-groomed gray mustache.

"I don't think you should worry much about this," he added, smiling broadly at me. "I'll write a few lines about what you told me and I'll give them to Officer Roos, so you can contact him if something else happens."

Art took a handkerchief out of the box on the table and wiped his forehead.

"How long will he be away?" I asked.

"I really don't know. A couple of weeks, maybe. Ask the clerk. But you've had enough of my time, my little friend, so it's time to go. There's nothing more I can do for you today."

He pulled a computer table toward him and took out a

bunch of paper that was on it. I sensed he was doing this to show me how overworked he was, so I got up to leave.

"Are you going to keep the letter?" I asked. Art shook his head.

"No, take it," he said without looking up. "It'll be fine. Thank you."

I had been dismissed and made to feel ridiculous, but I just got up and walked out to the clerk. The woman was so busy talking to a dark-haired guy leaning over her desk that I gave up waiting to ask when Andrew Roos would return. I put the letter in the outer pocket of my backpack instead, and ran to catch the bus.

I missed the bus home, so I had to sit at the central bus station for almost half an hour to get the next one. This got me even more annoyed. I bought a horse magazine and some candy, but soon gave up reading the magazine and sat people-watching and eating my candy.

The bus finally arrived. I hopped on, showed my bus pass and then sat down to read my magazine. The magazine had a long article with a bunch of beautiful photos about a riding tour to Andalusia, Spain. I wished that I had the money to go there right now. I could imagine myself escaping the gray, cold autumn weather for Andalusia's roasting hot sun and tons of beautiful horses!

When the bus came to a halt at my stop I had almost completely succeeded in forgetting about the letter. But when I stepped onto the gravel road and started the short walk toward home all the unpleasant feelings returned. I looked around carefully, and stayed vigilant the entire walk home. A little off the main road there was an old deserted army camp. I hurried past the overgrown garden and avoided looking in the dark, empty windows. At first the woods were very close and dark, but they soon opened up as the road bordered some farmland. Our farm is behind Hans and Maggie's, which I could now see and, relieved, I took a deep breath. *How silly can I be*? I thought to myself. I'd safely gone down this road a million times before without a single problem …

Everything seemed normal, I thought as I hurried along the road. The fall sky was cloudy and I could smell damp earth and rotting leaves in the ditch beside the road.

There was a light on in our kitchen window, and I hoped with all my heart that someone was home. When I walked in the house and saw Sophia sitting in the living room watching a Julia Roberts movie, I was so relieved. I made a snack for us, with hot chocolate and sandwiches, and then I plopped down on the sofa to watch the movie for a while.

I had no desire to go out to the stable to care for the horses, and I didn't get up and go change my clothes until Dad opened the door and shouted that he was home.

It was raining and the horses were standing at the gate waiting. I pulled my collar up on my jacket and decided not to ride today. I mucked out the stalls very fast instead, and then gave the horses fresh hay and grain and let them in.

I tried to pretend everything was just as it usually was. Even so, I jumped when the barn cat came pouncing down from the hayloft. And when Fandango kicked the wall to protest Winny getting fed before him, my heart skipped a beat and then took a few extras. But nothing else happened, and I was soon on my way back to the house. At the dinner table a little later, I complained about how much homework I had, and Mom promised to go out to the barn later that evening so I wouldn't have to care for the horses again.

After dinner I went up to my room, sat at my desk and took out a textbook. Never before had it felt so nice to be inside doing homework instead of caring for the horses, I thought. I picked up my cell phone and stared at the display. I had a text message, and with trepidation I clicked on it. To my relief, it was from Molly, who wanted to speak with me. I saw that she'd tried to call me a few times, but because I had the ringer off I didn't realize it until now.

I went out in the hall, got the telephone and dialed her number while sitting on my bed.

Molly was home and quickly came to the phone. She hadn't ridden today either.

"Dad and I are going to go to the racetrack this weekend, since we have a new horse that will be running his first race. Do you want to come with us?"

"Oh, definitely!" I said. "That'll be great! I've never been to a harness race in my life!"

"You've made my day!" Molly said happily, but then she got quiet.

"What's the matter?" I asked and heard her suck in her breath.

"Unfortunately, George is going too," Molly said slowly. "I know you don't like him … but George always goes to the races. Last weekend, for example, he and Dad went to race Black Babe and another young horse."

Suddenly I didn't know what to think. To be in George's company for the whole day – did I really want to do that?

On the other hand, I thought, it would give me a chance to try to find out more about what he was hiding. Not that I wanted to play detective, but I couldn't stop wondering why he was behaving so strangely.

"I'll still go," I said quickly, and tried to sound happier than I felt. "It'll be fun!" I added with an excited voice.

"Great," Molly said, and I could hear the relief in her voice. "You know, Dad loves it when I go with him. He hopes that I'll follow in his footsteps and become interested in harness racing."

We changed the subject, complained a little about school, and then I hung up and put the phone back in the hallway.

I could feel butterflies in my stomach whenever I thought about the weekend to come. Why in the world had I said yes? Why was I so darned curious? Couldn't I just leave it for someone else? No wonder I get myself in hot water time after time. Sometimes I really should put the blame on myself.

Chapter 9

The next day Mom picked me up at school. She drove the long way home past Ridge Farm and the cottage where George lived so we could buy some meat at a small farm shop out that way.

I sneaked a look at the little red cottage when we drove by. I could see the blue light of a computer screen through the window, and couldn't help but wonder what George was looking at. I'd have given a prize to the person who could tell me which URL he was visiting.

I sat quietly almost the whole way home – so quietly that Mom finally asked if something had happened. Nothing really had, at least nothing specific ...

"I know you're unhappy that Mike might have to move away," Mom said when we'd driven a while. "I thought everything would be okay once he and Hans had talked and cleared the air, but that obviously didn't happen."

"Mike's tired of being used," I answered briskly, because I had no desire to discuss this with Mom.

"And you're really sad about it. I understand!" Mom

tried again, but I just stared out the window without saying anything. Couldn't she see that I was in no mood to discuss this with her?

"You know that you can always come to me and Dad if there's something wrong," she continued. I knew she was just trying to be nice, and was taking advice from the usual magazine articles about what parents of teens should do: "talk about the problem," "participate in the teen's everyday life" and nonsense like that. But the only thing I could really tell her for sure was that I was in a bad mood.

And besides – what can Dad and she do to get Mike to stay here? Hire him to work on our little farm? Hardly.

There's nothing I can do, except wait and see if he finds another job. The alternative is for me to get used to the idea that he's leaving – and our relationship might not survive the move …

"Sara," Mom said in a friendly voice, "say something. How're you holding up?"

"Hello, hello, don't you get it that I don't want to talk about it?" I shouted, annoyed. "Leave me alone!"

"All right," Mom sighed as she turned into our yard and parked the car. At least we were home …

"Fine, thanks for the ride," I said curtly, jumping out of the car and slamming the door shut. I didn't want to talk to anyone, so I went right up to my room and threw myself on the bed.

I got my cell phone out of my bag and saw that Mike had sent me a text message. But instead of calling him back, I shut my cell phone off and turned off my bedroom light. Then I just lay there in the dark and cried for a long time. Nothing was any good! What if Mike really did move away? … Darling Mike who I loved with all my heart! How could I manage without him?

And then there was also that strange business from last week. That curious letter. The unpleasant, threatening George with his piercing eyes.

Darn it – I had no desire to go to the racetrack over the weekend. I kept thinking up excuses, each one better than the last to get out of going – but I had to forget all the excuses for one special reason: Molly was my friend, and I couldn't let her down.

After a while I sat up and turned on the light by my bed. A chilly autumn wind blew through the tree outside my window. I got up and decided to take a warm bath. But first I looked at what Mike had written in his text message. It was just a few words, but they put me in a much better mood.

"Have a job in the works. Call me when you get home! Hugs," was all he'd written, and I hurried to call him. But Mike didn't answer. Just then someone knocked on my door and I shouted, "Come in!" The door opened and there he was!

We hugged each other, and then Mike happily began to tell me about the job he was trying for. It was as a horse caretaker at the town's riding school, and it seemed tailor-made for him. He would work in the barn and give some lessons. The stable director had seemed very positive about his application.

"Fantastic!" I said, and hugged him again. "But are there other applicants?"

Mike shrugged his shoulders.

"There's definitely one other person interested, but when the director and I talked it sounded as if she was thinking of hiring me immediately, so I'm not too concerned about it!"

Mike looked so happy, and I thought that it was unbelievable how everything could be resolved so easily.

Mom shouted from the bottom of the stairs, "Hello up there, Sara and Mike, do you want dinner?"

Suddenly I felt as hungry as a wolf, and we were soon packed in around the kitchen table with Mom, Dad and Sophia. The food smelled wonderful, including a huge pile of hamburgers in the middle of the table that Dad had just grilled.

After dinner, Mike cleared the stable while I took a short ride with Fandango. Later the family watched a good movie on TV, and Mike stayed to watch. In spite of the fact that the movie was really good, and that Mike sat next to me on the sofa, I ended up getting really irritated. It was Sophia's fault – she was acting like a busybody the whole time. She was speaking with a fake grown up voice to Mike, and talking only to him – as if they were the only two people watching the movie and I was some totally unknown and uninteresting person that she didn't even recognize.

And besides, she babbled a whole bunch of nonsense the whole time! She commented on the actresses, their clothes, movements, asked Mike about other movies he'd seen with Tom Cruise, told Mike about some interview she'd read in some magazine, blah, blah, blah … Finally, I got so tired of it all that I told her to be quiet for a while.

"Why?" Sophia blurted out, shooting me a dirty look. "I don't talk very much!"

"Huh!" I replied with irritation. "You've been talking nonstop! I want to hear the movie, not you. That's why I'm sitting here watching it!"

"Mike, do you think I talk too much?" Sophia turned to Mike and asked him in a fawning voice, which put him on the spot.

"No, no ... well, maybe a little," he said trying to dodge the bullet. I knew he didn't want to be unfriendly to Sophia or to me, and he also didn't want to get in the middle of a fight.

And that really made me angry! Why couldn't he just say to her, "be quiet"? I was sure that he was just as tired of her incessant babbling as I was.

I pulled my hand away from his and got up.

"I'm going out to give the horses their dinner," I said while Mike looked surprised.

"Aren't you going to finish watching the movie?" he asked.

"I've seen it before," I said. "Who cares?"

I went out to the hall to get my stable clothes on without waiting for Mike. Our black lab Swift came bouncing up to me. He loves to go out and visit the horses, and I patted him on his head.

Swift was always happy, no matter what happened.

I heard Mike say something to Sophia, and then he came out into the hall.

"I'm coming with you to do the horses," he said, putting on his jacket. "Then I really have to go home."

"You're welcome to finish watching the movie if you want," I said in a sulky voice as I pulled a heavy sweater over my head. "As long as you like to hear Sophia yammer through the whole thing."

The last thing I said was really a little unnecessary – and I can admit that now – but at that moment I was so mad I wanted to spit out anything hurtful.

"I don't like it any more than you do that she talks the whole time," Mike said calmly to me. "But can't I at least be polite about it?"

"It's wasted on her," I said opening the front door. "C'mon, Swift!"

The wind was very cold, and I shivered despite my thick sweater. I should have taken a jacket instead. But who cares if I'm cold, I thought as I went toward the barn, feeling sorry for myself.

Mike caught up with me and put his arm around my shoulders.

"Why're you in such a bad mood?" he asked, perplexed. "I thought you'd be happy that I might have a job!"

I didn't answer right away. He really was right – I should've been very happy, but instead I couldn't help feeling that everything was out of control, hopeless and sad.

"You're not even sure you've got the job," I muttered. "You shouldn't celebrate before it happens."

Mike opened the squeaky stable door and Fandango began to kick his stall door with his front hooves. He likes to do that to let us know that he's super-duper hungry, and make sure we won't forget him!

"Quiet, you," I said angrily to Fandango, but as usual he didn't care one bit and just continued to bang.

I sighed and mixed the grain with vitamins while Mike gave the horses hay.

We kept working without speaking, and when the horses

finally had all they needed and calmly stood chewing their hay, Mike pulled me over to him.

"I have to go home," he said, "but first, will you tell me what's bothering you?"

"Everything," I mumbled. "You're on the outs with Hans and are going to move. I get a strange, threatening letter in the mail. Molly's dad's horse trainer is nasty to me every time I go there, and this weekend I've committed to going with Molly and her dad to the racetrack, even though I don't want to because George will be going. Isn't that enough?"

"What?" Mike said and held me at arm's length looking at me carefully.

"Then you shouldn't go to the racetrack," he said shaking his head. "I have no idea what George has against you, but he doesn't seem to have all his marbles. There's no reason you should subject yourself to the nasty remarks of that idiot."

"But I promised Molly that I'd go," I said. "She'd be so disappointed if I backed out, so I feel obligated."

Mike looked at me thoughtfully and then said, "If I went too, would that make it better?"

"Do you really mean that you'd go with me?" I asked in disbelief, and all at once it seemed like the weight of the world was lifted from my shoulders. "I wish I'd thought of that earlier!"

"Of course, it's no problem," Mike said smiling at me. "Hans can't say anything because I did so much extra work during the summer."

Suddenly it felt like the weekend wouldn't be horrible after all. Oh, I am so lucky to have such a wonderful boyfriend!

Just then Swift barked and ran toward the stable door. His hackles were raised and he growled, and both Mike and I kept still, listening.

"Someone's coming," Mike whispered.

"Yeah!" I whispered back, as I felt my mouth go dry.

Swift growled softly again – the door opened with a creaking noise, and … there stood Dad!

"So there you are," he said happily and stepped into the barn. "I saw the lights on and thought I'd make sure the horses had their evening meal," he continued while petting Swift, who was circling around him wagging his tail. Swift seemed a little embarrassed – after all, he'd just growled and barked at his beloved master, and not a dangerous scoundrel!

"We just fed them," I said, smiling at Dad.

"Great," Dad said, yawning. "C'mon now, let's go. It's getting late and tomorrow is a school day."

We left the barn together, turned out the lights and went back to the house. Dad went in first and Mike took his bicycle and starting riding home. I watched him pedal out of the yard and onto the gravel road with his bike light showing the way in front of him. Way ahead of him I could see the lights from Hans and Maggie's house, and I took a deep breath. I wondered how it would feel to have some-one besides Mike live in the little cottage on their farm. And what if Mike didn't get the job at the riding school?

With that thought I felt the lump of anxiety return, and with heavy steps I went inside, shutting the door behind me.

Chapter 10

The weekend came upon us quickly, and I managed to feel both excited and uneasy. On one hand it would be awesome! I had never been to a racetrack before, even though this one was only a few miles away. On the other hand – I wished George wasn't going with us. As soon as I thought about that part, I got a stomachache.

On Saturday, Mike picked me up right after noon and drove me to Ridge Farm. Molly was helping her Dad pack all their gear, and George was in the stable with a young and beautiful light brown horse. The horse stood on cross ties while George put wraps on his legs.

I must be honest and admit that even though I didn't like George I understood why Molly's dad thought he was so talented with horses. The young stallion pranced nervously the whole time, but George never raised his voice or seemed the least bit stressed. He talked calmly to the young horse, patted him on his neck and coaxed him to relax, and before the horse knew what was happening he was wrapped in transport blankets and leggings and ready to load.

The little transporter stood with its doors open toward the barn door, but the young horse wasn't going anywhere near it – he made that clear. He threw his head, snorted and danced around. But George made no big deal out of it. He was just as calm as before, and let the young horse continue prancing. Mike offered to help, but George just gave him a patronizing look and shook his head quietly. And soon the horse calmed down and walked right into the transporter without any more trouble.

George shut the doors, and then he and Eric jumped in the truck cab and Eric waved good-bye to us. I noticed he had a large gauze bandage around his right hand.

"Dad got bitten by one of the young stallions yesterday," Molly said as we got into the back of Mike's car. "He was leading him in from the paddock and the horse tried to play with Dad and ended up biting him by mistake," she continued.

"That's bad luck," I said, and Molly agreed.

"Yeah, there's so much to do around the farm, and George won't do a bit more than he has to. Even Dad's getting tired of him. It's lucky, though, that Dad isn't hurt worse, so he can still drive the truck."

Mike started his car and we slowly followed the swaying horse trailer out of the yard and then onto the gravel road. I was so glad that Molly sounded just as happy as I felt.

It didn't take very long to get to the racetrack. Soon we were waiting outside the gates, right behind the truck, and we were waved into the stable area by a heavyset old man in jeans with red suspenders and a plaid shirt and cap.

There was lots of lively action at the stable. The young horse, whose formal name was something long, fine and unpronounceable, was called Vincent. He let out a loud whinny from inside the truck, and the other horses responded.

After we parked the car we went over to the truck where George was unloading Vincent and leading him to his stall, one in a long row of simple outside open stalls under one roof. Vincent was nervous about everything, and he whinnied again like crazy. Some of the others answered, but most of them didn't seem to care about the newcomer's loud cry.

Eric went to the registration office to make sure all his papers were in order, and Mike asked George again if he needed any help. George hardly answered him this time either, but he did mutter a "no." George then began to take the race sulky from the back of the truck where it had been hanging.

"We're not very popular here," Mike whispered to Molly and me, nodding toward George. "C'mon, let's take a walk."

We looked around for a while, but there wasn't a lot of stuff open to the public. Molly said that she'd noticed that was typical at the many tracks she'd been to.

There were one or two great horses racing tonight, and they were mixed in with all the others. But there wasn't one in the same class as Black Babe and the really elite pacers. Most of the people here were owners, officials or horse trainers – of course, there was also a group of men (and some women) who were placing bets.

We met Eric on his way back to the stable, and he suggested that we get our seats early so we'd have a good view of the track. We each bought an ice cream cone, and then found a good spot along the sideboards at the finish line.

Race One was announced over the loudspeakers, and the horses burst out onto the track. They were long-legged, elegant, and all different shades of brown. The first race was for youngsters and wasn't very fast – at least Molly said it wasn't. But since I'd never seen a live harness race before I thought they were going extremely fast when they crossed the finish line.

Vincent was starting in the fourth race, and about 45 minutes before his race we headed back to the stable. There he was, standing in his stall half asleep. Molly looked around, confused.

"Where're Dad and George?" she asked. "It's way past time to harness him and begin his warmup!"

"Warmup?" I asked with surprise. Molly smiled at me.

"We always let the horses warm up before a race, exactly like you do before show jumping. Some need more, others less, and I know Vincent's the type that needs more. He ought to be on his way out with his sulky by now!"

Eric came running into the stable. He looked around anxiously, and sounded stressed when he asked if we'd seen George, which we hadn't. Eric made an angry scowl and searched the stable.

"This horse has to get out to the track soon, or he won't be in the race. I bet George is sitting and having a drink somewhere … darn him!"

"I can help," Mike said calmly. "My dad used to have a couple pacers. I know how to harness him, so you won't have to do it, and I can warm him up, too."

Eric looked Mike up and down for a second, as if he were measuring him.

"Okay. Unfortunately, I can't really help because of my

hand … but you probably won't have to warm him up. The driver usually does that when it's a young horse."

We took Vincent out of the stall and Mike quickly began to put the harness and protective leggings on him. Vincent had a halter with side blinders, and he had two bits in his mouth, a very small one and a slightly thicker one.

Vincent would not stand still for a second, but Mike was just as calm as George had been earlier. Just as the driver came over, Mike fastened the last strap to the sulky – and Vincent was good to go.

The driver was an older man with a gray mustache and probing eyes. He had a friendly smile, and he patted Vincent on the neck.

"And how's this fine creature feeling today?" he asked in a broad drawl while Mike straightened the halter for the last time.

"Just great," Eric answered. "He's mighty strong, but still unsure in certain situations …"

Eric and the driver chatted about Vincent and the race for a few minutes, and then the driver took the reins, hopped up in the sulky and they rolled away toward the track. Mike was in front, holding Vincent's halter. Vincent was tense and nervous.

"It makes Vincent feel safer, having Mike at his head," Eric told me.

We three followed after them at a slower pace. Eric looked around the whole time, and when we got to the track he sighed deeply and shook his head.

"I still wonder where George is hiding. Where in the

blazes can he be? He's always here when a young horse runs his first race."

It wasn't yet time for the start, but soon the pacers began to gather behind the start car. The announcer called out the names of the various horses in the race, but I hardly recognized Vincent when he trotted by us. The lanky young horse that had been prancing around just a few minutes ago had now transformed into a long-legged racehorse with only one thing on his mind – coming in first over the finish line.

"He's an awesome driver, that Johnson," Molly said and nodded toward the track. "He's driven tons of young horses, and Dad always begs him to take ours. He's kind to them, but pushes them to win."

I nodded, and at that moment the start car sped up and the horses began to run after it at a faster pace, and then they were on their way!

The announcer told us what was happening in the race, but he spoke so fast that it was hard to decipher what he said. On the far stretch we couldn't tell which horse was which – it was just a flock of brown horses with sulkies behind them that came rushing forward, swaying from side to side.

"Darn, I forgot my binoculars at home," Mike muttered to himself as he stood beside me. "We can't see a thing …"

The horses were still all clumped together late in the race, and I wondered where Vincent was. Was he in the middle of all the others? Or was he last? I was afraid he was, because the last place driver's jacket was just like Johnson's.

But I was completely wrong! When the horses trotted

into the last turn, a light brown horse was pulling ahead in front. Quickly, he pulled even farther from the others with long strides. Soon he was a couple of lengths in front of his nearest competition!

"VINCENT!" Molly screamed. "It's Vincent, out in front!"

"Yes," Eric gasped, sounding like he could hardly breathe from excitement. "Yes it is, I don't believe it … He's ahead!"

Vincent had a big lead, and we were sure he would win, but suddenly there was a challenger. A darker brown horse surged forward from behind! With his ears flattened and huge thundering steps he drew closer to Vincent, who seemed to be giving it his all to keep the lead. With thundering hooves they neared the finish line and Molly, Mike, Eric and I screamed as loudly as we could! A few seconds later the two horses rushed by us and continued into the turn where they slowed down to a trot and then to a walk.

"What a race!" Eric panted and wiped his forehead. "Wow, I never thought Vincent was so fast …"

"Did he win?" I asked as Eric looked up at the large electronic scoreboard.

"I can't see it," he said peering at the board. "It must've been a photo finish."

"The question is, did he hold the lead?" Mike wondered. "But wow, how he pulled away from the others in that turn. That horse can really move!"

Eric nodded.

"With a little luck, he'll be really good in no time. With a little luck …"

95

We all walked back to the track's entrance, and there was Vincent, just as energetic as he was before the race. He held his head high and, except for being really sweaty, it didn't seem like the race had taken anything out of him.

"We won!" the driver said, and then grinned at Eric and us. "You don't believe it, eh?"

"The video will tell us soon enough," Eric said, patting Vincent on his wet neck. "Let's just cross our fingers for now …"

Mike undid Vincent's head strap, and Vincent threw his head around. He whinnied excitedly and took a few trotting steps. It seemed like he wanted to go around a few more times, if they would only let him.

"Yes, I know, you're always Mr. Cautious, Eric," the driver said, smiling again. "But you know me, I can always tell when we've won …"

Just then the scoreboard blinked, and Vincent's name was on top! He won!

"Unreal!" Molly screamed and threw her arms around her dad. "He won, he won!"

Eric looked overjoyed as he strode onto the track with Vincent and the driver to receive the prize. They hadn't won a huge pot of money, but from what I saw today, I thought this might be the beginning of a new harness racing star's career.

Molly glowed with happiness as we went back to the stable. Mike held my hand and I looked at him happily. What a great day this had been! I still couldn't believe Vincent had won!

"Wish we could have bet on him," Mike said when we

were back in the stable and the driver hopped out of the sulky and gave the reins to Mike. "He paid eleven to one!"

"Well, ha," John said. "There'll be other opportunities. This is a great horse, most definitely!"

He gave Vincent a quick pat, then took off Eric's racing clothes and waved good-bye to us.

Just then the track veterinarian appeared with his assistant. They said they had to give Vincent a blood test for illegal drugs, and I shot Molly a glance. Drug test?

"It's normal procedure," she said to me as the vet went into the stall. "Every time there's a race, they check a certain number of horses."

"Okay," I nodded. "I didn't know that."

It took a while for the vet to get a sample, so we went back to the track and watched the next race. Mike put his arm on my shoulders while we stood watching, and as usual I felt so lucky to have him. My boyfriend, my Mike – how would I manage without him if he had to move?

I buried that thought and decided to push all negative thoughts away for now. I just couldn't manage to think about all those problems now. I wanted to enjoy the day, to enjoy standing with Mike, looking at the beautiful horses out on the track. To feel happy for Molly and her dad, now that they have a new winning racehorse in their stable … I just wanted to live in the moment and feel every happy thing.

We went back to the stable, and the vet was just finishing up. Eric had already started to gather up Vincent's gear.

"George is still missing," he said, looking at the clock. "This really isn't like him," he said anxiously. "If he hasn't shown up by the time we're ready to go home, I'll ask them to call his name over the loudspeaker, and talk with the guards to find out if they've seen him leave the track."

"Molly and I can take a walk around and look for him," I suggested, and both Mike and Eric agreed.

Okay … I wasn't particularly fond of George, but I couldn't help it that Eric's worry had spread to me. And as we went around looking for him Molly mentioned several times that it wasn't like George to just disappear.

"He has a bad side, as you know," Molly said while we passed the almost empty café and a horse racing shop. "But George is great with his horses, and he's always looked after Vincent well … this just doesn't make sense."

We searched and searched, but couldn't find George anywhere. Finally Molly suggested that we go behind the grandstands and check there before going back to her dad and Mike.

The last race had just begun, and we heard thundering hooves as a clump of horses went by. We could hear the loudspeaker even this far away, and a cold burst of wind was sending all the papers and waste left on the gravel swirling around. But George wasn't here either, so we went back to the stable again.

We went over to Eric who was standing by the trailer, ready to open the side gate. He looked questioningly at us, and Molly shook her head.

"We've searched everywhere, Dad. He isn't anywhere."

"Okay," Eric sounded tired. "Let me think about what we're going to do. While I'm figuring out something we can pack everything in and be ready …"

Suddenly he stopped what he was saying. The back gate was now completely open and we could see right into the trailer – and there was George, leaning comfortably against a hay bale with his long legs stretched out in front of him. He was deep asleep, snoring with an open mouth, and his cap had slipped at a slant.

"Well, isn't this something!" Eric said angrily. "Get up, George! Get up!"

But there was no reaction from the horse trainer. He snored louder, deeply lost in his dreams.

Now Eric lost his patience. He grabbed Vincent's water bucket and poured the entire contents on George! George groaned and came to, then moved himself a bit and opened his eyes.

"You idiot!" Eric snarled at him. "Is this where you've been the whole time? You're supposed to be working!"

George said nothing. He just yawned a big one and looking at Eric with piercing eyes.

"We're leaving – now," Eric ordered, and George got down from the truck bed, swaying his way to the cab.

We quickly loaded in all the gear and Vincent into the truck and fastened the sulky onto the back.

"Fire him," Eric muttered angrily to Mike. "I'm going to fire him … Just wait!"

And I knew from Eric's voice that he really meant it.

When we arrived back at Molly's farm, George sulked off to his cottage. Neither Eric nor Mike cared to bother with him. Mike helped out with Vincent and unloaded everything from the truck, and then he and I offered to stay and help out with everything that needed to be done in the stable.

Eric thanked us for our offer to help. As luck would have it, he still didn't have a full barn, although he had signed up quite a few horses for training. At the moment there were only about ten pacers; most of the rest were young horses on their way to becoming pacers, and they were out in the large pasture. Some of them needed to be brought in for the night, including the young stallion that had bitten Eric a few days ago. Mike led him in, and I was on the verge of telling him to be careful – but then remembered that Mike had grown up on a large farm with several breeding stallions . I assumed that he knew what to do with a young stallion to keep from being bitten like Eric had.

The stable chores didn't take very long, but Eric was still grateful for all our help. He couldn't do very much with his injured hand, and it sure didn't look like George was going to be much help this evening.

"I hope he's planning to work in the morning," Eric said in a worried voice when we'd finished and were ready to go home.

"Give me a call if you want me to come by tomorrow to help," Mike said. "Hans's horses are still outside and I can definitely sneak away for a few hours."

Eric and Molly waved good-bye to us as we drove out of the yard, and then I leaned back against the seat and shut my eyes. It had been a long day, and I felt absolutely exhausted after all that had happened.

Mike let me off at my farm and then drove off. At first I didn't want anything to do with my horses – it had been a long day. But after I lay on the sofa for a while, I got some energy back and decided to take Winny for a ride in the woods. It would be our first ride alone ever, and this was a calm, beautiful autumn afternoon, just perfect for a ride.

Unfortunately, Dad had other ideas. As I reached the stables I turned around and sighed, watching him coming in hurried steps from the house. He had that no nonsense aura about him – and I knew exactly what that meant. Dressage, dressage – and more dressage!

Chapter 11

I called Molly on Sunday morning. She told me that her dad and George had had a terrible argument out in the stable earlier in the morning.

"I thought that George was going to punch Dad," she said, and I could hear from her voice how frightened she'd been. "George threatened Dad several times, and said that Dad should watch out or George would see to it that something horrible happened, and a bunch of stuff like that."

"That's awful," I said. "What'd your dad say?"

"He told George to go home and take a nap. That made George angrier, and then he started to muck out the stable. But he was so furious that he kept throwing pitchforks full of dirty straw next to the wheelbarrow the whole time. I didn't dare stick around any longer, so I went into the house. I hope he doesn't go after Dad or do something awful …"

"I don't think he will," I said and tried to sound more confident than I felt. "It's one thing to threaten someone, and entirely another to do something. But what's your dad going to do now?"

"I don't know," Molly said and drew a deep breath. "Mom and I are trying to get Dad to understand that he has to fire George, and not care whether George pays him back the money or not. But Dad's as stubborn as a mule. He wants George to do right by him, and besides …"

"Besides what? I asked.

"I think he's afraid that Black Babe won't run as well if George doesn't care for her. She's really attached to George and, no matter how stupid he is, Black Babe is still the apple of his eye. And he would never hurt her," Molly added.

After I laid the receiver down I thought about how strange George was. He was such a nasty, untrustworthy person, and yet he was incredibly fantastic with horses and could get an unwilling mare to give her all on the track. I could understand why Molly's Dad was having second thoughts about firing him. Eric had known George for many years, long before he became the bitter man he is now …

Several days went by. I had tons of schoolwork, but I still found time to ride both Fandango and Winny every day. I tried to get Fandango to think dressage was more fun by first taking just a few rounds and then by riding a short piece on the track before giving him his dinner.

Dad and Josie thought that changing gaits and gymnastic exercises were important, so I worked the most on those – although it didn't go very well. One evening I did seven galloping exercises in a row – and Fandango refused and bucked at every one! I didn't think Josie and Dad were right about his training …

I also took Winny for a short ride on the track each evening, although it was obvious that she didn't like to be out when it started to get dark. She spooked at things that she usually didn't care about, and even though the night-lights were on, it didn't seem to help. Then she was afraid of the shadows instead! But when she behaved well, her gait was smooth and even, and almost every ride had a few brief moments of that fantastic feeling I had the first time I was on her back.

On Thursday it was time for my jumping lesson again, so after school I hurried out to the pasture and brought Fandango in. It was very windy and the sky was a nasty gray. I thought that it was unbelievable how quickly the cool weather had moved in. Just a few weeks ago I was riding in my tee shirt and it felt like summer – now it was definitely fall.

I got Fandango ready and then went to get Dad to drive us over. As usual, he was sitting in front of a computer re-pairing something, and when I came in he looked up and seemed confused.

"I'm ready," I said. "Aren't you driving me to the lesson?"

"Oh, no!" Dad shouted, running his hands through his hair so it stood straight up. "It's not working."

"What's not working?" I asked with surprise. "You know it's Friday, my usual lesson day."

"The car's not working," Dad sighed. "Joe's coming tomorrow, and we'll try to get it going again."

Dad's car is probably the world's most repaired car,

and we never know when something will go wrong. Dad's brother Joe can usually fix it, but both Mom and I have told Dad at least a thousand times to sell the car and get a new one.

Mom has a car too, but it's just a little Toyota and definitely can't pull a horse trailer.

"What should I do?" I asked, both sad and irritated. "It's almost time for the shows and I have to train for them!"

"Can't you jump here at home?" Dad asked, trying to sound encouraging. "Mike could help you!"

"It's not the same thing," I snapped. 'You know that!" Dad sighed and looked guilty, and I turned on my heel and marched out into the kitchen. Sophia was sitting there, reading a book and drinking tea. I poured myself a cup and sat down.

"What's wrong?" Sophia asked. "You look like you've just gone seven rounds."

"I'm supposed to have a lesson and the car's broken – again," I muttered and stirred some honey in my tea. "I'm so frustrated about missing the lesson."

"Can't Mike come and drive you and Fandango?" Sophia asked, but I just shook my head.

"No," I said. "He doesn't have a hitch on his car. And he'd never be able to borrow Hans's big car, especially the way things are right now ..."

Sophia nodded.

"Yeah, Hans is a real pain."

She gulped some tea and got quiet.

"But," she suddenly said cheerfully, "can't you get a ride with Molly?"

"Yeah," I hadn't thought of that. "Molly!"

"Yeah, she goes to the lessons with her horse. They could easily drive you and Fandango to the riding school."

I jumped up.

"Thanks for the suggestion!" I said gratefully. "You're an angel!"

I rushed over to the telephone and dialed Molly's number. Fandango and I could probably go with them easily. They had to drive by our farm, and Fandango was a breeze to load.

Their phone kept ringing, and I drummed my fingers nervously on the telephone table. Finally Molly answered and I explained what I wanted.

Of course, Molly sounded very happy to help me, and said it was no problem for them. We could go with Little Brother and her to the lesson. She would just ask her parents while I waited on the phone for an answer.

It took just a minute before she was back, and she didn't sound as happy as before.

"George is driving Little Brother and me to the lesson today," she sighed. "I really don't want him, but Dad isn't home and Mom won't drive the horse trailer."

As she said this, I instantly regretted calling her. But at the same time I couldn't back out, so I told Molly that it didn't matter. The heck with it, it was just a short drive. What could happen?

"I'm glad you're coming with us," Molly said cheerfully. "You know I don't like him either."

"I hope he's awake," I said.

We agreed on the time they would pick us up, and hung up.

106

I was sorry that I'd called Molly – but at the same time I was glad that Fandango and I could go to the lesson. *I'll just have to make the best of it*, I thought to myself, and went back out to the kitchen to drink my tea.

An hour later Fandango stood in the stable passageway, ready to go with his bridle, blanket and leggings on. I had just bought the blanket a few weeks ago – a thin sweat blanket in dark blue with white edging. It matched Fandango's varied gray coloring, his blue halter and leggings perfectly. I usually don't care about matching colors for my horses, but when I saw the blanket in the tack shop I just couldn't resist buying it, even though it emptied my wallet.

Just then Molly's horse truck turned into our yard, and I sucked in my breath. I couldn't help feeling nervous but I tried to get rid of that feeling as best I could and happily called out "Hi" to Molly.

George didn't seem very happy to see me – he looked as if he'd just seen a rat in the grain storage bin. Without a word he opened the back so I could lead Fandango in next to Little Brother. We tied the horses so they wouldn't be able to get in each other's way, but Little Brother neighed loudly anyway.

Molly smiled. "Sometimes he thinks he's still a stallion," she said, patting him on the nose. "Little man …"

"Hurry up, will you!" snapped George and looked at his watch. "We don't have all day!"

I put my saddle, bridle and safety vest in the truck's small tack room, and then grabbed my helmet and got into the cab beside Molly.

We sat in absolute silence the whole ride to the school.

107

George's sullen face spoke volumes what he thought of our company, and neither Molly nor I had any desire to talk when he could hear us. The wind was blowing hard outside. I put my arms around myself in a big hug, wishing I'd taken my nice warm jacket.

When we got to the riding club, Molly and I were the first in the indoor ring, so we went to see if Josie needed help building the jumps. Our group was the only one that jumped on Friday nights, so we usually set up our own obstacles.

The club was actually an old indoor ring that some-body had put an addition on, so the whole building was 250 feet long. That meant that it was big enough for two rings, and the riding school could give lessons at the same time the private horse trainers worked in the other ring.

The building hadn't been cheap to construct, and to keep our riding costs down almost all the members of the club and their families had helped with the construction somehow. I hadn't really done much, but Dad had spent a lot of time there, nailing boards and painting. He'd also installed the sound system, and made sure the club had an adequate computer system for its bookkeeping.

We went to the back of the truck and let the horses out. Fandango had succeeded in untying the knot on his halter, and stood loose, but luckily for me he hadn't made any mischief.

Fandango gave a good look around when he came out into the stable yard. He had his bridle under his halter, and I quickly attached his reins. I knew how he could behave sometimes, and I wanted to make sure I had something besides the halter to grab. I held him with one hand and at the same time tried to get the saddle out of the small tack room with the other. Molly was already saddling Little Brother, and George was standing with his back to us, looking at the riding arena.

Fandango seemed to think I was taking too long, and he began to shift around. I grabbed the reins and told him to stand still, but he must have thought I was silly, because he snorted loudly and threw his head.

Just then a fancy car with an elegant horse van pulled into the courtyard. "BUSY BEE" was written in huge letters on the van's side. Fandango decided to act scared of the car and trailer as it passed us, and I almost lost hold of my saddle.

"Darned horse!" I yelled and couldn't help but notice George casting us a glance and grinning.

I yanked on the reins, and told my wild pony to behave, but that didn't help much. He just bobbed his head up in the air and pranced around even more.

Molly was already finished with Little Brother, and she watched us uneasily.

"Do you want some help?" she asked, and I shook my head.

"It'll be fine," I mumbled, and put the saddle on again while Fandango stared as Fredrik unloaded Busy Bee from the horse trailer.

This time I had a little more luck, and I was able to tighten the girth and put the saddle on Fandango. Next I put his martingale on and, after making sure everything was in place, I tightened the girth another notch, put my foot in the stirrup and hoisted myself up.

"All set?" Molly asked, and I nodded.

"He seems wild today," Molly said as we walked toward the arena, and I nodded.

"It's really windy. He's usually extra frisky when the wind's blowing," I said, patting my pony on the neck.

Fandango, who must have heard what I said, shied away from a trash can that he's seen about a thousand times – and then he crept into the riding arena right on the tail of the well-behaved Little Brother, acting like he'd never been here for a jumping lesson before.

Once we were well inside my pony looked around as though he'd never seen an obstacle or the arena. When I urged him to trot slowly along the square track he went into a balanced trot with his head and tail held high.

"What's with him?" asked Josie, smiling as I rode by. "He seems full of it today!"

It's the wind," I said, and took a turn around her. "He'll get better when we start the jumping."

Fandango snorted and threw his head forward, so I did a quick halt and slowed down to a walk. I knew him all too well – that was usually the sign of at least two more real bucks, and I wasn't going to let him buck me off! As luck would have it, Fandango didn't try to buck, but instead he began to walk diagonally to avoid the 'dangerous' outer wall where the wind could be heard like small sighs.

I sucked in my breath and patted my pony on the neck. He was absolutely hopeless when he behaved like this! Usually I'd just laugh at him, but right now I was aggravated. I had no desire to have George or Fredrik's dad laugh gleefully if he decided to buck – and it would be dangerous to hang on if Fandango kept this up …

Everyone began to ride around the ring, preparing for

some of the low jumps. I threw a quick glance at Molly and Little Brother. Little Brother wasn't jumping any better than he did last time – but there was still a big difference between our two horses, and Molly had more control over her horse. I couldn't help but feel good – Camigo had been able to teach her a lot in the one time she'd ridden him! Now she dared to let Little Brother have more speed before the jump, so they got a better lift and she had an easier follow through.

I was up next with Fandango. He steamed, snorted and tugged at the bit in a foaming frenzy. Suddenly he took a couple of steps to the side, and almost lost his balance. I did a half stop and then drove him forward – ordering him to sharpen up and pay attention so we could take the jump!

Josie had built a nice little track that started with two obstacles along the long side, then there was a turn to the left and an oxer. Then we would go across the riding ring, turn to the right and jump over one more oxer. I was glad there weren't two high jumps, one after the other. The smaller jumps were no problem for Fandango …

But just then Fandango did a humungous buck! I felt my stomach leap into my throat, and then my horse exploded under me in a series of leaps and back kicks that even the best rodeo rider would have found difficult staying seated! In spite of my effort to stay on, I was thrown from the saddle and landed on my back in the sawdust with a heavy thump that took my breath right out of me.

I lay absolutely still and looked up at the arena's ceiling, my head spinning around. Then I succeeded in taking a couple of breaths and sitting up. Josie came running over and told me to lie still, but I didn't want to do that. I wasn't hurt, just breathless. I quickly got up on shaky legs and looked for Fandango, who had trotted down the arena. I was entirely covered with sawdust, and I tried to brush it off while Josie went to get Fandango.

Fandango was standing in one of the farthest corners of the arena, scraping the sawdust with his front hoof with irritated concentration. Then he began to turn around to lie down, and I saw that he was totally wet with sweat on his neck and sides.

"No!" I screamed and rushed after Josie – I had absolutely no desire to see him roll around with my expensive jumping saddle on his back!

But before I could get there Fandango folded his front legs and lay down.

"Get up!" Josie hollered, and Fandango snorted again and got up on all four legs. He was shaking and quivering terribly, and I rushed to grab the reins that were strangely still, hanging over his neck.

"What happened?" Josie asked and I shook my head.

"I don't know," I said. "I can usually stay seated when he bucks. But this one was totally unexpected!"

Josie patted Fandango on his neck in a calming way and made small talk with him while I fixed the bridle. But inside I knew there was something really wrong with him – I had this gnawing feeling of impending disaster.

We went in toward the center of the arena and suddenly Fandango stopped. I turned around toward him and saw his whole body quiver! Sweat ran off of him and he was breathing in short, jolting breaths. His eyes were wide open and I could see the whites of his eyes. I thought he had a strange, almost glassy-eyed look. Suddenly he tried to throw himself to the side! He raised himself up on his hind legs, which was so unexpected that only my survival instinct allowed me to hold onto the reins. Then he backed up a few steps and reared up again on his hind legs with his front hooves moving like a fan right in front of my face. I threw myself to the side and again my survival instinct kicked in and I avoided being hit.

"I'll take him!" Josie said and grabbed the reins. "Hey, calm down, boy …"

But Fandango just continued to back up while he pulled Josie with him by the reins! He pulled and pulled on the bit, froth standing like a white cloud around his muzzle. And his eyes … his look was dark and strange, and he threw his head every which way – with the whites of his eyes gleaming.

Suddenly he rushed forward and seemed to jump right at Josie. Then he turned, went down on his knees and fell right in front of me! He snorted and kicked, lying on his side, rolling here and there in the dusty shavings. I stood like a statue, unable to move, and watched him, unable to understand what had happened. It wasn't until Josie grabbed me by the arm and pulled me back so I wouldn't get hit by the swirling hooves that I finally understood. Fandango was dying right there in the arena, dying right before my eyes!

"No," I screamed … "Nooooooooo!"

Chapter 12

I have no idea how long it took. Maybe two minutes. Maybe four or five. But it felt like hours had flown by while we stood there, staring at Fandango as he threw himself uncontrollably forward and backward in front of us.

The sweat ran off him, he kicked non-stop and the whole time he had a strange, glassy look in his eyes.

I was sure he was going to die. I would've gone to him – but Josie wouldn't let go of me. She told me over and over that I needed to wait, be patient, and not get near him …

There was nothing I could do for him, she said – and the risk of being kicked or crushed when Fandango threw himself around was just too great!

The other riders stood away from us with their horses. The riding lesson on the other side of the wall had stopped too, and I saw some small girls peering over the wall as they sat on their ponies. Some parents came into the arena and rushed over to Josie and me.

Slowly, Fandango began to calm down. He kicked a few last times, and then lay stretched out on his side, looking relaxed, with closed eyes. His breathing was heavy and wheezing, and it sounded like he didn't have too many minutes left to live …

"I'm so sorry, Sara," Kate's mom said as she put her arm around my shoulders. "Just stay calm and let Josie go to him first!"

Josie kneeled down by Fandango's head and carefully patted him on his muzzle. He didn't open his eyes, but just continued to lie absolutely still. He didn't even react when Josie said his name.

"He's dead," I cried, and Kate's mom hugged me harder.

"No, he's not," she said in a comforting voice, but I heard in her voice that she wasn't sure whether he was dead or not.

"Somebody call the vet, please!" Josie said, and Kate's dad held up his cell phone.

"I've already done it," he said. "Now I'll call Sara's parents. Sara, what's your number?"

"What?" I said in my confusion, and blankly stared at him without really seeing him. "Number? What number?"

"Your home telephone number, honey," Kate's dad said, sounding like he was talking to a small child.

I looked at him, but couldn't answer. My head was empty, and if someone had asked me my name right then – I'm not really sure I could have answered correctly.

Suddenly Molly stepped forward, leading Little Brother, and she rattled off the number quickly.

I just kept staring at Fandango, who seemed completely lifeless. He kept his eyes shut and showed no visible signs of movement or life.

115

I knew that he was going die. I just knew it! I sniffled and knew it was too late to do anything for him now …

But suddenly, a shiver went though his entire body. He kicked with his legs, took a deep breath – and opened his eyes!

"Fandango!" I cried. "Please … don't die! You can't die!"

My beloved horse moved his eyes as if he heard me. Then he lifted his head and gave a little snort before he rolled over and tried to get up. It was as if his legs couldn't support him, yet he managed to get up, and staggered around a bit. He looked incredibly tired, and hung his head and breathed unevenly. I couldn't stay away from him any longer. I got loose from Kate's mom and rushed over to him. He raised his head, looked at me with his big brown eyes, and buried his head in my arms, as if he was asking my forgiveness for what he'd done.

Each passing minute still felt like an eternity. We all stood there in the middle of the arena and waited for the vet and my parents. Someone got Fandango's blanket from the truck and put it over him. He wasn't sweating any more; now he was shivering like he was frozen, and wobbling back and forth.

"Should we try to lead him into the stable?" Kate's mom asked, looking at Josie.

"Yes, that's a good idea," Josie answered and nodded. "We've got an empty stall just now. He can have that one."

"What should the rest of us do?" Fredrik asked as he came walking up with Busy Bee. "Is there going to be a lesson, or what?"

"If we can move Fandango then you can all ride," Kate's mom said. "If you still want to?"

116

"I don't want to," Molly said quickly. "I'll put Little Brother in the trailer for now."

She led Little Brother toward the exit while Kate and Fredrik continued to ride around on their ponies in another section of the arena. Kate's dad came to help me take Fandango's saddle off. It had gotten scratched in the frenzy, but it didn't seem to have suffered any real damage.

Josie came back and said that the stall was ready and I led Fandango slowly toward the front of the arena. The stable was built almost flush with the arena, so we had to go outside for only a short distance. Fandango walked with unsteady steps, and now and then he sucked in a deep breath and shook his head.

Josie put us in a corner stall after she shoveled in a bunch of clean wood shavings. Fandango stumbled when he went over the threshold, but as soon as he was in the stall he stopped and stood with his head down and eyes closed. He was breathing better now, and seemed disinterested in the world.

Just then Mom and Dad came into the stable. Both of them looked anxious, and Mom put her arms around my shoulders and gave me a quick hug.

"My poor baby, are you okay?" she asked, and I nodded silently.

It felt so good to have my parents there; safe, secure and comfortable.

"What happened?" Dad asked, stroking Fandango on his neck, which was caked with sweat and sawdust.

"I don't know," I said, and heard how my voice shook. "I was riding, and he seemed really energetic. And suddenly he went completely wild – threw me off, and …"

My voice cracked as I sniffled, and I had to wipe tears from my eyes.

"Then he threw himself down in the sawdust and just lay there, kicking," Molly filled in for me. "It was the worst thing I've ever seen!"

I nodded.

"I thought he was dying!" I sobbed, and Mom hugged me again.

"Poor baby …" she said, and I wiped away my tears. I was shaking and felt like my legs would no longer hold me up. I sunk down on a hay bale that was against the wall in the corridor, and buried my face in my hands.

"This is a shock reaction," I heard Mom say, her voice sounding like it came from someplace far away.

A few minutes later the vet arrived. It was Dr. Fransson, the same vet we use at home for our horses. He's tall and thin with gray hair, and at the moment was wearing a grim expression.

"How's he doing?" was the first thing he asked, and then he saw Fandango, still standing with his head down.

"I don't know for sure," Dad said, "but he seems out of it. Like he's been drugged."

The vet and Dad went into Fandango's stall, and I got up on my shaky legs and went over too. I wanted to hear what the vet had to say.

He had me tell him everything that had happened one more time, which I did it. I felt the shock reaction ease as I explained it all in detail. And when I saw the vet, with his experienced hands, examine Fandango, I began to hope that things weren't as bad as I'd originally thought.

The vet listened to Fandango's heart and lungs, felt his

legs and took his temperature while Dad held Fandango's head. Not that it was necessary – he just stood there like a very tired old horse, with no energy to care or protest.

When the vet had finished his examination he looked carefully at Fandango.

"He must have gotten into something," he said, stroking his neck. "But what? And even more importantly – how? Has he been someplace by himself lately?"

I shook my head.

"I came here with Molly," I said, with a nod toward my friend. "Her horse, Little Brother, and Fandango shared the same trailer, and we checked on them the whole time. Everything was totally normal until he started bucking and kicking."

"Wait a minute," Molly said. "He was really agitated when you saddled him, jumping around and acting fidgety. He's not usually like that, right?"

I thought back and tried to remember when it began. I knew that Fandango could be a brat sometimes, but had this been worse that his usual naughtiness? It was hard to say! Maybe, maybe not …

But I remembered the feeling I had when I started to ride into the arena. Fandango had been unusually crazy, I thought. Spooked and unwilling to go forward …

"Well, was that how he really was?" the vet asked, seriously searching my face. "How was he to sit on, right before it happened?

"He usually makes noises in the beginning," I said slowly. "But he was worse than usual today. Like … I wasn't able to make contact with him!"

The vet nodded and looked at Fandango again.

"He's absolutely been into something he shouldn't have," he said slowly. "The question is, what, and who gave it to him? You're absolutely certain he was never alone?"

"Yeah," I said, nodding, but then thoughts began to swirl around my head.

Fandango drugged? How could that have happened? I tried to think clearly, but it was as if I couldn't make sense out of it. It was just so unlikely and unbelievable – this whole thing …

"But you must have left him alone somewhere for a few minutes. Are you absolutely sure you didn't …" insisted Dad, and at that second I knew what had happened!

"When we got here, Molly and I went into the club-house to see if Josie needed help setting up the obstacles," I said. "The horses were alone for a short time inside the trailer. I forgot about that …" I continued, shaking my head.

"It's because you had a real shock," Mom comforted me. "Sometimes you can't remember the whole sequence of events, only parts of them. Then in a little while, as the shock subsides, you can remember more and more."

Dr. Fransson nodded in agreement.

"Okay, I'm going to take some blood and run some tests," he said. "I'm not sure we'll find out much, since we don't know what we're looking for, but we can always hope that it'll give us a lead."

He took a test tube and a disposable hypodermic needle from his box, and Fandango – who usually hates all shots and needles – stood stone still while the vet filled three tubes with blood.

"He's really depressed, your pony," Carl Fransson

said, and gave me an encouraging smile. "Normally he'd be trying to get a hundred miles from here."

I couldn't help but return the smile, in spite of the whole horrible situation. I thought of all the times over the years that Dr. Fransson had difficulty vaccinating Fandango for influenza, for example. One time he got loose and knocked the vet over, ran out of the stable and around the garden for 20 minutes before I was able to grab him … Ouch, that was a painful memory!

"I'll send these samples to the lab," Dr. Fransson said, putting the test tubes in a little holder. "But don't count on any clear answers. We may not find anything at all."

"Hey …" I said suddenly… "I just remembered another thing. When we came back to the horse trailer after we'd been in the clubhouse, Fandango was loose in the trailer. He was standing there eating hay in the hay rack; he'd untied the knot with his teeth."

"You mean that …?" Dad said and stared at me, and I knew he was thinking exactly the same thing.

"I think there's something funny about the hay," I blurted out.

"Let's look," Carl Fransson said as he shut the stall door on Fandango – and we all hurried out of the barn and over to the trailer.

When we got to the trailer Dad stepped up in the horse van part with Dr. Fransson on his heels. Dad was just going to stick his hand in the hay when Dr. Fransson stopped him.

"Wait! I have latex gloves in my car. I'll put them on so we don't risk destroying any evidence – if we find something there."

We nodded while Dr. Fransson hurried out to his car to get the gloves. But Dad couldn't resist searching further. He took Molly's riding whip, which was hanging in the tack room, and began to carefully poke between the hay strands.

Just then a tall skinny man came running out of the stable. It was George! He stopped dead, gave us an uneasy look, and then rushed over to a little red car that was parked beside the empty passageway outside the riding school's office. He threw himself in the car, slammed the door, stepped on the gas and drove away so fast that gravel spun out from under the tires. The car disappeared down the road with the motor roaring.

A young woman came running out of the office, screaming, "My car! He's stealing my car!"

"What in the world!" Dr. Fransson shouted. He looked at the woman and then asked us, "What's going on?"

"It's our Manager on the farm. He drove Sara and me here today," Molly explained.

"But why'd he take my car?" the woman shot back. "Why?"

Dad suddenly yelled from inside the truck.

"Everybody, come over here. There's something strange ..."

We hurried over to the truck and I peeked into the hay bale. Then I heaved a deep sigh, and felt an ice-cold hand squeeze my heart. Down at the bottom of the hay was an opened plastic bag, half-filled with pills.

Chapter 13

When Dr. Fransson came back with his gloves. Dad had already called the police and, to my great delight, it was Officer Andrew Roos who arrived in the big police car.

He was obviously back from vacation, and when he caught sight of my parents and me, he raised his eyebrows – and then gave us a broad, teasing smile.

"What have you gotten into now, Sara?" he asked, and I really didn't know how to answer. It was as if he thought I liked having a bunch of strange things happen to me all the time!

We told him what had happened, and he scowled. After we had finished the whole story, he went into the trailer and searched carefully under the hay, in the hay bag, and the rack. Just as Carl Fransson had done earlier, Officer Roos now put on latex gloves so he wouldn't destroy any clues or evidence. He whistled to himself – and then stepped out of the truck and took off the gloves.

"It's stuffed full with every possible suspicious-looking substance down under the hay," he said. "There are plastic

123

bags with both powder and pills. One of the bags is broken, and I guess that horse of yours ate some of the contents, Sara. And now I have to ask – who owns this truck?"

"My dad," Molly said guardedly, her face turning white. "But … he's not guilty! I know it!"

"Don't worry," Mom said, putting a protective arm around Molly's shoulders. "No one is accusing your dad of anything."

But Molly looked ready to burst into tears, and I felt really sorry for her.

"We'll have to get some technicians out here to gather all the evidence," said Andrew Roos's partner – a young woman with long light brown hair. "I'll call the station," she continued. "And we'll need to talk to your parents, Molly."

"Are you going to confiscate the trailer? If so, how will we get the horses home?" Dad asked Andrew Roos.

"I'm sorry, but I'll have to take the trailer, and we can't help transport the horses. Isn't there another horse van you can borrow?"

"Our car's broken," Dad heaved a deep sigh. "Unfortunately …"

"Molly's horse can go home in our van," said Fredrik's dad, Frank Carlson, clearing his throat. "We've got to go that way. And your horse ," he said turning toward Mom and Dad, "should probably stay here overnight, don't you think?"

I couldn't help but stare at him with a surprised look. Mr. Carlson wasn't exactly known for being helpful to anyone – but maybe he'd changed his ways, after what happened this past summer …

"Okay," whispered Molly, and I knew she was holding back a sob in her throat. "That's so kind …"

124

"No," Andrew Roos said, "I want your horse to stay here for the night, if we can get a stall for him. The fewer people walking around your farm right now, the better it is for my technicians."

Molly looked frightened, but she nodded quietly.

"And now I hope you'll write up a report about my stolen car!" the young woman angrily said to Andrew Roos's partner, Officer Lena Danlund. "It's at least as important as all the other messes, which have nothing to do with me."

"We'll take care of it," the policewoman answered calmly, taking out her notepad and a pen. "Tell me what happened …"

The young woman started to talk – but didn't get very far before Andrew Roos interrupted her.

"Are you saying that the guy who drove this trailer here is the same guy who later stole your car and disappeared?"

"I … I don't know," said the woman. "I only know that my car disappeared! I went into the office to hand in my application for the upcoming shows, and I left the car standing by the walkway outside the office. It's been difficult to start lately so I left it running with the key in the ignition since I was just handing in an envelope, and …"

"Does anyone else know who it was?" Officer Danlund asked, and I nodded.

"Yes, it was the same guy," I said. "His name is George, and he works for Molly's parents."

"Okay, and your name please?"

"Sara," I replied.

Just then a police car drove into the stable yard, followed by an unmarked car. To my surprise the chubby policeman that I'd met at the station was driving the car. He didn't seem to recognize me, so I didn't say 'hello' either. Two technicians hopped out of the unmarked car, and immediately marked the trailer off-limits with plastic tape that had "POLICE" written on it.

"Where do you think he went with my car?" the young woman asked me. "If you know him, maybe you know where he went?"

"I don't know him, exactly," I said, "but …"

"That car means everything to me!" she announced sternly. "I have absolutely no money to get another, and if he crashes it … well, he can't! I've got to get it back!"

She became even more upset, in spite of Officer Danlund's efforts to calm her down. The officer told her they'd probably find the car parked someplace nearby, and she'd certainly get it back.

"Okay," Andrew Roos said with a deep sigh. "We now have a mess of leads to get started on. Lena and I will drive to George's cabin and try to find him there. He has a whole bunch of things to explain. And you, Art," he said to the older pudgy policeman, "you go get a search warrant for both George's cottage and Molly's parents' farm … And there's a huge hurry!"

Just then Molly's parents drove into the stable yard in their other car, and now it was their turn to hear what had happened. I knew that I couldn't listen to all that babble one more time, so I went in to see Fandango, who was still standing half asleep in his stall.

I went inside, leaned against his warm flank and shut my eyes. He breathed deeply and I felt the tears well up in my eyes. He was alive, but he could just as well have been dead … that thought got me really shook up.

A while later Dad showed up outside the stall looking for me. He came in and patted Fandango on the neck. My most beloved pony was slowly getting some energy back, and I was so happy to see him start to look for pieces of hay in the wood chips.

"At least we now know how he got the drugs," Dad said, and I nodded.

"Yeah, he's always searching for goodies. He must have ripped the bag with his teeth just to find out what was in it …" I said, patting my adorable pony on his neck.

"It'll be interesting to know what it was that he ate," Dad said as he gave Fandango a friendly caress on his muzzle.

"Narcotics, I bet," I said. "White tablets in plastic bags – what else can it be?"

"Medicine, maybe," Dad offered seriously. "They smuggle in medicines in powder form or as pills and pack it later before they sell it via the Internet. It could be anything … including just plain flour! The people who buy things through shady sites over the Internet have no idea what they're getting in the mail."

All of a sudden a thought smacked me in the head – that page I had seen on the Internet! The page that George had been so interested in – what was it called? Yeah, "Pill Dealer"! I thought about what had been going on up in Molly's hayloft, and how Molly and I had – we had actually wondered what George was hiding up there. I bet he had his hiding place up there in the hay the whole time! And just a few weeks ago he was in another state with Black Babe, who was competing in a huge race … Had he gone over the border and brought back drugs, and then sold

127

them on the Internet? Suddenly the puzzle was coming together, and I was getting a clear pattern!

Just then Mom showed up outside the stall. She said that we had to drive down to the police station and give our statements. Then we could come back to visit Fandango if we wanted to.

Josie, who had come into the stable with Mom, had already agreed that Fandango could stay until tomorrow, and even longer if necessary. It was no problem at all, because the stall was empty, waiting for a new riding horse that Josie had bought. And there was also another stall that was free for Little Brother, so he could spend the night too.

I gave Fandango a big hug and then went on wobbly legs out to the car, trying to remember everything that had happened during the last week.

The police station business took a long time. We had to give our statements one at a time in a little room, and tell everything that we knew to an old policewoman, who wrote it all down on a pad. I told her all about George's strange behavior, the home page he'd visited on the Internet, and the threatening letter I had received. The policewoman didn't comment on anything, but just wrote down what I said.

When everyone in our family had finished giving their stories, the lady in the reception area told us we could go home. We were getting ready to leave when Molly's dad walked into the room with the policewoman who had taken our story. He was as white as a ghost, and when he saw us he sighed and shook his head.

"I'm afraid I can't go home just yet," he said to us. "They want to keep me for questioning."

"But …" my mom said, but she didn't get another word out before she was interrupted by the policewoman.

"Unfortunately," she said with a firm voice, "you may absolutely not speak with anyone. This way, Eric."

She put her hand on his arm, and with a bowed head he went before her through another door.

Just then Molly and her mom arrived, without a police escort. Molly had been crying, and her mom had her arm around her. She was just as white and hollow-eyed as her dad had been, and I guessed something must have happened that we didn't know about.

"They've taken my dad … But he didn't do … it isn't him. He didn't put it there! It was George!"

"I know, I know," said Molly's mom as she hugged her. "Everything will okay, you'll see. They haven't even charged him with anything. They only want him to answer some questions."

But I knew that she was very worried. She had a troubled look in her eyes, and I felt so sorry for her.

"I think you should come home with us," Mom said and put her hand on Jane's shoulder. "Come, you shouldn't be alone at a time like this."

"But the horses …" Molly began, but my mom interrupted her calmly.

"They're all outside, from what I understand. There's lots of grass to eat, and I'll get Andrew Roos to have the police take care of them. And I'm sure Little Brother will be fine at the riding school."

At first Molly's mom looked as if she wanted to

protest, but then she nodded weakly and we all went to our cars. Dad drove Molly's parents' car, and Molly and her Mom went with him. I went with Mom in our car.

The last thing I noticed at the station was the young woman whose car was stolen talking to one of the officers who worked behind the desk in the lobby. Her mouth was moving nonstop and she was gesturing wildly, so I knew she was talking about her stolen car. I sincerely hoped she'd get it back – it must be horrible for her to be an innocent, involved in this whole thing.

When we got home, everything seemed normal, and my horrible day felt like a dream. Winny, Camigo and Maverick were grazing, quiet and calm in the cool fall weather.

Molly and I went out to the pasture and talked to the horses. Winny came forward in a friendly way and rubbed her head on my arm, while Camigo nosed Molly in the stomach so she lost her balance.

"You brat," she said, and couldn't help but smile. "Maybe I'll ask the police to take you in, too!"

"You don't think your dad's involved, do you?" I asked carefully. "Stop me if you don't want to talk about it."

"He couldn't be," she said, sucking in her breath. "It's impossible! Daddy's the most honorable man there is. He only tried to help George with his gambling addiction, and … George is so gifted with horses! Why didn't George get it … that horses are more important than gambling away all his money …"

I shrugged my shoulders.

"He can't help it," I said. "It's a disease. If a person isn't ready to change, then he can't be cured. And even if he wants to be free, it's easy to fall back into the old habits again."

Molly nodded.

Just then Mom came out and called to us. She had made dinner, and inside the house smelled like fresh baked bread. The kitchen lamp shone its golden light over the table. It felt safe and secure to be home, and I tried to calm myself and trust that everything would work out for the best.

Of course the police would find Molly's dad not guilty! But if they didn't, what then?

Just think, if he weren't innocent?

Chapter 14

Molly and Jane slept at our house. Sophia was curious about everything that had happened – and a little jealous that she wasn't in on it, since it sounded so romantically exciting.

The next morning at breakfast, she started to talk about it for at least the tenth time since last night.

"But I wonder what was in the bags?" she pondered, as she put sugar on her corn flakes. "Imagine, Fandango being drugged! No wonder he got so wild – I've seen it on TV, how they …"

"Stop it right now!" I snapped. "It wasn't the least bit funny, seeing him lying on the ground, kicking. I was sure he was going to die. Why do you have to keep talking about it?"

Molly looked down at her teacup. Sophia's face turned beet red, and there was a painful silence. I realized that I could've been more diplomatic, but sometimes I just get so tired of Sophia! I felt a little ashamed, though, having made such a fuss …

"I'm sorry I got so angry at you," I mumbled. "It was silly. But everything still feels so horrible, with Fandango and … everything …

Sophia didn't say anything, just scowled, then got up and took her crutches.

"Mom, can you drive me to Alexandra's, please?" she said.

Mom sighed.

"Sure. I have to go out and shop for the week anyway."

Sophia nodded and then hopped out of the kitchen. I could hear her thudding up the stairs.

"It's okay," Jane said, patting me on my hand. "We're all upset. We can only hope that the police catch the guilty party as soon as possible."

"Yeah," I said, feeling my face get red.

"And you know," she added, "even though I'm terribly anxious, I know Eric's innocent, and that's the most important thing. And Molly knows it, too."

"You ought to call the riding school and see how Fandango's doing," Mom said and I nodded.

"I already did," I replied. "I have Josie's cell phone number, so I called her before breakfast. Dr. Fransson was there again this morning and examined him, and he's much better today. And Little Brother is out in the paddock eating grass, just as calm and happy as can be."

"That's great," Jane said with a smile.

She answered her cell phone, looking anxious again. With quick steps she walked out of the kitchen so she could speak in private. After a few minutes she came back into the kitchen.

"We can go home now, Molly," she said. "The police

are finished in the house. They're still going through the stable, so Little Brother has to stay for a while longer."

"Have they found anything?" Mom asked, just as curious as I was.

Molly's Mom was silent, then she said quietly, "Yes, I hate to say it … Up in the hayloft they found lots of cartons with bags of pills and other … It's … It's so unreal!"

She was shaking, and drew in a deep breath.

"But at least they know that Eric wasn't involved," she continued. "We're going to pick him up on the way home. But George has disappeared. The car that he stole is parked by his cabin and his own car is gone."

I saw a tear roll down her cheek and she swallowed before continuing,

"I kept telling Eric that he shouldn't hire George, that he'd only cause us trouble … but Eric always wants to help people …"

She began to sniffle.

"And it seems that I was right … I was right all along!"

She sat down on the chair by the table and began to sob. Molly tried to comfort her, but she was just as emotional as her mom. Mom finally suggested that Molly and I go out for a walk while she talked in private with Jane, who was still sobbing.

Molly and I went out to the pasture. We didn't say anything, but just stood there petting the horses and making small talk with them. Winny was anxious for a cuddle, and I rubbed her all over her head and neck. Just then Mike drove up. He waved and stopped at the pasture.

"How's it going, you guys?"

He hopped over the wooden fence and came over to us.

134

"Not exactly great," I said. "Haven't you heard what happened?"

"No," Mike replied with a questioning look, and it occurred to me that I hadn't spoken to him since the afternoon before our lesson.

"I tried to call you last night," Mike said, "but your cell phone was turned off. You'll find exactly seven text messages on it when you turn it on."

"Oh," I said weakly, turning red in the face. "I forgot all about my phone ..."

We sat down on a fallen log in the front pasture, and Molly and I took turns filling him in on all that had happened. Mike looked very serious and nodded now and then. For the most part he said nothing, but just sat quietly.

"What a shame that they haven't found George yet," he said when Molly had finished, and she nodded.

"Yeah," Molly said and it sounded like she was going to cry again. "Just think, if they never catch him! What if they believe that it was my dad who ..."

"There must be a mess of evidence," Mike said, soothingly. "Fingerprints, and such. Everything will be all right!"

Molly sniffled again and nodded, but I knew she wasn't really sure. And I wasn't so sure, either. I felt angry and frustrated – how could someone do what George had done? How could George let a kind man like Eric take the blame for his mistake? I simply couldn't understand how a person could behave that way.

Just then Jane and my Mom came down the steps together. They looked at us and Mom called to us. We walked over to them. Molly's mom was ready to go home to their farm, and she asked if Molly wanted to come along. She was much calmer now, even though her eyes where still red and her breathing was a bit ragged from crying.

"Can we go see Little Brother on the way home?" Molly asked, but her mom looked at her with a tired face.

"Do we have to? I don't really feel up for it," she said sadly. "Can't we go this afternoon instead?"

"I can drive the girls over to the riding school," Mike said. "And I'll drive Molly home after."

"Will you really do that? That's so nice of you!" Jane said gratefully.

"Yes, that sounds like a very good idea," Mom agreed – and so we piled into Mike's car.

A while later we drove into the riding school's courtyard in Mike's little car. It was quiet and still in the stable, but out on the riding track Josie was just finishing a beginner lesson for several young children on ponies.

When the lesson was over, she came over to us.

"Hi," she said with a happy grin. "Fandango's much better. And Little Brother is out, grazing over there," she added to Molly, pointing to the riding school's spare pasture.

There hadn't been any horses in that pasture all summer long, and Little Brother looked very happy, tasting all the fresh green grass.

Fandango had started to act like his old self again, but he was still exhausted. He chewed slowly on some hay, and Josie said he had been drinking gallons of water. He whinnied when he saw us, and spent a long time sniffing me all over to make sure I really didn't have a pocketful of goodies for him. He seemed to say that he deserved goodies, because he'd been sick!

Molly went out to visit Little Brother, and when she came back to the stable she called her mom on her cell phone.

"Mom wants to know if I can go back to your house with you," she asked.

"Of course you can," I said back. "Do you want to?"

Molly nodded.

"I guess it's horrible at home. The police looked through the whole house, and turned everything upside down. And they're still looking through the hayloft.

"Did they find George?" Mike asked, and Molly shook her head.

"No, he's gone like a puff of wind – and he took his computer with him. But they've set up roadblocks on all the major roads and sent out his description, so the police don't think he'll get far."

After a while Mike drove us home. No one was there. Dad was at work, and Mom had gone off with Sophia. Molly and I sat down in the sunshine on the porch. Neither of us said anything, but I knew we were both thinking the same thing … how awful this all feels! And where was George? What will happen when they find him? I tried not to think about it …

I wanted to find something to take Molly's mind off the situation. There had to be something better to do than just sitting and stewing over the situation.

"Do you want to go riding?" I asked, and Molly looked surprised.

"Riding? Now? Why? I don't know if I …"

"We can ride up in the woods," I suggested. "You can borrow Camigo."

Molly hesitated as I got up to go.

"We'll just take a little tour. C'mon. You even have your riding clothes on!"

And that was true – Molly was still wearing the clothes she had on from yesterday's lesson. Molly followed me slowly out to the pasture and helped get Winny and Camigo in. My stomach felt a little uneasy. Mom wouldn't be happy if she knew I was taking Winny into the woods! But then, I reasoned Molly and Camigo would be with us. Nothing bad could happen, I thought, in an effort to convince myself that it was true.

A little while later we mounted up and rode out of our stable yard. As we got farther from home, I began to lighten up and feel better .

Molly seemed happier, too. Since Camigo needed prodding to go along at a steady pace she was forced to think about something other than the mess at home. Winny, on the other hand, walked calmly, and I thought to myself what a fantastic, wonderful horse she was. Every time I got the chance to ride her, and gaze at her thin neck and long pointed ears, joy just bubbled up inside me. It didn't matter that she was difficult sometimes – I loved her all the same!

"Where should we ride?" Molly asked when we came to the edge of the woods, and I got a bright idea.

"I can show you the shortest way to your house," I said. "The one I told you about before. It's an old logging road that goes right straight through the woods. I've never gone the whole way, because I thought the gravel road was the shortcut to your place."

"Sure," agreed Molly with a nod.

"We don't have to go all the way to your farm, if you

don't want to," I added. "We can stop at the gravel road and turn around again."

We shortened our reins and began to trot. Camigo labored on with eager steps while Winny stretched out into a comfortable trot. She pulled at the bit, but it felt soft and okay, and I thought maybe Josie and Dad were right – there's nothing wrong with doing a little dressage every now and then.

We soon arrived at the gravel pit, and I showed Molly some great sandy paths where we could have an excellent climb and gallop. We tried one of them, and Winny took off like a racehorse along the path. It ended on a hill, and I loosened the reins and let her gallop as fast as she wanted while I just enjoyed the speed and strength of her long leaps. When we stopped the horses on the crown of the hill, Molly laughed loudly and patted Camigo on the throat.

"That was awesome!" she enthused, and I was glad that even though things were so horrible at home Molly was a bit happier now. It had been a great idea to go out riding.

We turned onto the logging road. It wasn't as wide here, as the woods had begun to fill in again. The woods grow fast, I thought, once the loggers are gone.

At the beginning, the road was very uneven and had huge potholes, and we let the horses walk with long reins so they could choose their own path. But soon the ground was better, and I thought how strange it was that I'd never bothered to follow this path before.

We began to trot again. I soon heard Camigo go into a gallop behind us and I let Winny do the same. She understood what I wanted and began to gallop with long, comfortable strides. Camigo snorted behind us. I knew that he wanted to run and jump like Winny, and guessed that Molly was having a tough job holding him back. I smiled to myself.

Suddenly, Winny came to a dead stop, and I thought I was going to do a front somersault over her head. If she hadn't tossed up her head and started to focus on something in the bushes by the edge of the path, I wouldn't have had a chance of staying on her back. Camigo came to an abrupt stop too, but Molly was more prepared and had no problem staying in the saddle.

"What is it?" I said softly, patting Winny's neck. She felt as tense as a violin string, and I could feel her heart beat against my leg.

Camigo wasn't as upset as Winny. He didn't seem to care much about what was ahead! He took the opportunity to steal a few leaves from a nearby birch tree.

"Come, now," I said to Winny. "What do you see, little lady?"

"There's something wrong," Molly said and pointed. "Look … there's a car in the bushes!"

Now I saw it, too! I could just make out the back part of a rusty white car sticking out of the bushes. There were long, churned up tracks in the logging road's grassy surface, which showed that the driver had been going at high speed, lost control and crashed right into the tree that stood in the middle of the bushes.

I heard Molly suck in one gasping breath after another.

"That's George's car!" she announced. "I'm sure it's his!"

Chapter 15

We rode up to the car and got down from the horses. My legs were shaking, and Molly's face was pale and showed she was just as afraid as I.

The car was halfway into the bushes, and I couldn't see if anyone was sitting behind the wheel or not. I thought I could see a head, and took a few hesitant steps nearer to get a better look.

"We should see if he's still in the car," I said to Molly, who shook her head.

"I don't want to go there," she said in a soft voice. "Can't you? I know I'm being silly, but I … I just can't."

"I'll do it," I said, and gave her Winny's reins. "Here, hold Winny, please."

I felt my legs buckle as I reluctantly moved toward the car. My heart was beating frantically, and every second seemed like an eternity. All I wanted to do was get up on Winny and gallop away as fast as her legs could carry us! But at the same time, there was something pushing me to at least take a look. If George was still in the car, he was probably hurt and needed help. And the other alternative was one I refused to think about ...

With a shaking hand I bent a little bush out of the way so I could look in the car's side window – and I could see George in the car. He was lying, bent forward over the steering wheel, and my first thought was that he was dead.

"Oh, no!" I shouted, terrified, and put my hand to my mouth while I felt myself getting sick.

Suddenly, George moved. He opened his eyes, righted himself, leaned back and shut his eyes again. I took a few careful steps forward and opened the car door. I had to press up on it with all my strength, since the car was wedged between thick bushes. George sat upright, turned toward me and gave me a foggy look.

"Oh, help," he slurred. "I've driven off the road ..."

He looked and acted as if he were in shock, a feeling I understood well. "Just take it easy," I said in my most steady voice. "I'll call for an ambulance. How do you feel?"

"Dizzy," George said and drew in his breath with a wheeze. "And my legs ... they're trapped!"

He made a gesture toward his legs and I saw it was true. The crash had thrust the engine forward into the car, and it was now pinning him in. But it seemed strange that he wasn't really hurt and could move his legs a little.

"Have you tried to get loose?" I asked, but George just stared stupidly at his legs and then again at me.

"My legs are trapped," he slurred and shook his head. "I can't ..."

Molly had come up to the car with both horses in a rope train.

142

"Is he alive?" she asked anxiously, and I nodded.

"Yes, but he can't get out," I said. "We have to call for help!"

"Molly?" George questioned. "What're you doing here? Why …"

"I should be asking you that question," she snapped, and I could hear that she had gone from being frightened to angry in just a few seconds.

"What have you done, you idiot?" she raged as she tried to keep her voice steady, but I could hear her becoming more and more furious.

"Are you the one who put all those pills in our hayloft?" she snarled. "Was it you? You should know that the police have taken my dad into custody, and he might lose everything he's worked for … and it's your fault! You …"

She screamed out the last words and George crouched down during her attack.

"Yeah, but …" he began, but Molly interrupted him, and now she was in a full rage.

"Both Mom and I told Dad to fire you. We suspected that you were doing something that wasn't okay … but Dad is so kind. KIND! Do you get that? And because of that, you might have destroyed everything for us!"

Molly began to sniff in despair and then she slammed her fist into the car's roof as hard as she could.

"I hope you get what you deserve!" she screamed with tears running down her face. "Do you hear me? You've destroyed everything … EVERYTHING!"

"Try to calm down," I said taking Winny's reins, which Molly had dropped in her outburst. "Stay calm … everything will be fine …"

143

I really didn't know what to say, but Molly backed out of the bushes and began to sob, leaning against Camigo. I followed her out to the road, and then got out my cell phone and called the police. We were lucky because Lena Danlund answered directly, so I was able to explain a lot very quickly. She promised to come at once, and also to send for an ambulance and the rescue service in case George needed to be cut loose from the car.

I was still feeling sick to my stomach and shaky so I had a hard time giving directions to our location.

Then I called Molly's house and talked with her mom, and finally, I called my mom who didn't answer. She'd probably left her cell phone home on the kitchen counter, as usual. Dad's cell phone didn't work since he dropped it in a water barrel not too long ago, so it was no use calling him, but at least Mike answered. He promised to come as soon as he could, and once again I had to describe the way to get there.

I went to the car again and looked at George. He was leaning back now with eyes closed, breathing heavily. He had a deep cut in his forehead, and it had bled a bit. Otherwise he seemed relatively unhurt.

"How're you doing?" I asked, and he carefully turned his head toward me and opened his eyes. His eyes were watery, red-rimmed and swollen.

"I didn't want it to be like this," he said, almost pleading.

"Eric has always been decent to me," he continued. "But I couldn't ask him for more money … although if I didn't pay … they said they'd cut off her legs … Black Babe! My beautiful black pearl. The best horse I've ever cared for … I was forced to pay them!"

He took a deep breath and made a fist with his right hand, and then he hit the steering wheel.

"I should've turned myself in, you know … Instead I said 'of course, I'll help you' … although I hated it the whole time. But if I'd just gotten one big win, then I could have paid them off, and … But no. No, no! George can't win. George is always a loser … ha ha ha … the big loser!"

He closed his eyes and sniffled. A tear ran down one cheek and he dried it with a trembling hand.

I didn't say a thing, just stood quietly and waited. I didn't know what to do or say.

"I'm sorry about your horse," he said suddenly, looking at me with sadness in his eyes. "He's a good horse, that gray. He's okay, right? He didn't die, did he? I thought he might die … I didn't want that to happen!"

"My horse is alive," I said as calmly as I could. "In spite of you."

"I didn't want anyone involved. That's why I tried to keep you out of the hayloft. And then I wrote you that letter so you wouldn't come nosing around our place. After you came over, Molly began to seriously suspect something was wrong … do you get it? 'Watch out, Sara'…"

He drew a wheezy breath before he continued.

"Black Babe …" he said, and it sounded as if he could hardly say her name. "Now they've been paid, the devils. So they'll leave her in peace … I only sold what I had to! The rest I left in the truck and in the hayloft, and … I was thinking of burning it up. I swear! But … Poor Eric. What a fool I am …"

He leaned back, shut his eyes and drew a deep breath. Then he was quiet, and it seemed as if he'd fallen asleep.

We could hear the ambulance sirens from a long way off. We weren't far from the main road, and if I'd succeeded in describing the way correctly, they'd be here soon.

I went out to the road and over to Molly who still stood with Camigo. She was pale, her eyes swollen from crying.

"I heard the two of you talking," she said sniffling. "What'd he say? Did he try to explain …?"

I nodded.

"Yeah, he had gambling debts. Some people were going to hurt Black Babe if he didn't pay them off. So he paid … and got your dad involved. That's what he said."

"But he paid his debts," Molly said incredulously. "Dad gave him the money for that!"

"He must have gotten new ones," I said, patting Molly on the arm. "But it'll be over soon, Molly. I promise … it'll be okay!"

The police car slowed down to navigate the road and, right behind it, the ambulance and a red fire truck appeared. Winny began to get overexcited. She backed up and snorted, and her head bouncing up and down made me almost drop the reins. But I managed to hold on, and Molly and I took the horses away from the scene while the EMTs tried to free George from the car.

Lena Danlund came over to us, looking sympathetic.

"How's it going?" she asked in a friendly way. "Are your parents on their way here?"

"Mom's coming soon," Molly said, swallowing.

"My boyfriend should be here soon," I replied. "He said he'd pick Jane up on the way."

"Good," Lena Danlund said, nodding.

146

She stood with us a little longer while we watched the EMTs carry George out on a stretcher and lift him into the ambulance. Then they drove their large neon yellow van carefully away toward the main road.

"How're George's legs?" I asked. "He complained that he was pinned in. It didn't look too good …"

To my huge surprise, Lena Danlund smiled.

"His legs don't have a scratch," she said. "Thanks to the shock, he didn't realize that he just had to push the seat backwards, and he could have easily gotten out. It's pure luck that he didn't discover that, or he would have run into the woods and we might never have found him!"

The next day, Mike borrowed Hans's big car and his horse trailer to get Fandango and Little Brother. To my absolute surprise it was Hans who sat behind the wheel when they drove in to pick me up. He said 'hello' with a sullen face, but that was an entirely normal look for him, so it didn't bother me and I just said 'hi' back.

We were going to bring Fandango home, and that's all that mattered. Fandango was his old self again – finally! Agile like a young horse, he pranced around in the stable, and I hardly had time to get him ready and over to the horse trailer before it was time to load up. Once he was outside he trotted over to Hans's trailer and went in willingly. Molly came after us, leading Little Brother. Our two horses easily fit into the large trailer.

"I don't have a driver's license to pull this big trailer," Mike had told me as I put on Fandango's leggings for the ride home. "That's why Hans is driving."

"Nice of him," I said, and Mike nodded.

147

"There's nothing really wrong with him. He has a good and a bad side, just like everybody."

I smiled, feeling good inside, and hoped ... If Hans and Mike were friends again – maybe Mike could keep his job. It would be so wonderful if it could all come together.

We drove home slowly and began to unload Fandango. He went directly out to the pasture, and the first thing he did was to fold up his legs and lie down in his favorite place to roll. He's always loved to rub his coat with as much sand and dirt as possible. Then he got up, snorted like a wild stallion, and galloped diagonally across the pasture, bucking with joy. The other three horses watched him, and I guessed that they must have thought he'd gone crazy. He finally slowed down and began to graze beside the others.

"He sure is energetic and fit," Hans said, sounding friendly. "Now let's get Molly and her horse home."

"I'm going too," I said to Mom, who had come out when she saw us arrive with Fandango.

"Sure, do that," she said. "I'll keep an eye on the horses," she added. "Come home with Mike and Hans."

We got in the car and drove to Molly's house. There were several cars parked in front of the stable, including a police car and Molly's parents' car. The stable was taped off-limits with yellow plastic tape. I guess they were still looking for drugs in the hayloft.

We let Little Brother loose in the pasture, and he wandered around before starting to graze. He seemed completely at ease – as if a sleepover at a new stable was something he did every day.

We stood by the fence and watched him while a man came toward us.

"Dad!" Molly shouted and rushed toward him, throwing herself into his arms. He looked worn out, but his eyes beamed with happiness and he grinned broadly.

"Thanks for bringing the horses home," he said to Hans, offering his hand to shake. "I don't think we've met before. I'm Eric, Molly's dad."

Hans and Eric shook hands in a friendly manner, and then Eric turned to Molly.

"You don't need to worry anymore, Molly. Everything's been resolved. George took the blame for what happened, and I'm off the hook. It's ... well, it feels like a huge weight's been lifted from my shoulders."

"That's wonderful," Molly said, hugging her dad again. "What happens with George now? He's not coming back, is he?"

"No, I've had enough, I'm going to hire someone else, someone I can trust!" he said, and then added, "What luck that you found George."

Molly nodded.

"It was all Sara's idea to take a ride," she said smiling. "And when we were in the woods we saw a car that had crashed in the middle of some bushes. It was horrible, scary ..."

"At first we thought George was dead," I said, shuddering at the memory. "But then we discovered that he was alive ..."

"But what was he doing with his car on that little road through the woods?" Mike asked incredulously. "Not even Sara, who's lived here all her life, knew about that path until her dad told her about it a week ago. How could George know that it was a shortcut to the highway?"

"The way I see it, first he stole the car from the riding school," Eric said, "Then he drove home, parked it at his cabin and took his own car instead. When he pulled out on the road he probably saw the first police car, so he remembered the little road. We drove it together with my car a few weeks ago."

"But why? What for?" a surprised Molly asked.

"I thought we could use the road for training the horses. We needed to get an idea of how overgrown it was, so George and I drove almost to the gravel pit before we turned back. And if you look at a map, you can see that the gravel pit goes almost out to the main road."

"True," I said, nodding.

"What's going to happen to George now?" Molly asked.

"He's sure to get a long prison term, but first he's asked to be placed in a treatment center, as soon as possible. He wants to quit his gambling dependence. If he doesn't, he knows he can never have a decent life."

"What a waste. It sounds like he's a fantastic horse caretaker," Hans said. "It's a pity that he's had so many problems for so many years."

Eric nodded.

"Yes, that's why I gave him this last chance. He was the one who turned Black Babe into a winner, and without her we would never have had the money to buy this farm. She would probably have been a common riding horse, not a racer, and we'd never have been able to care for all the horses without George's help, either."

"Who're you going to hire to replace George?" Molly asked, and her dad smiled.

"I don't know yet. I'll put an ad in some horse newspapers, and then we'll see what we get. It'll work out."

"I'm looking for a job right now," Mike said calmly. "I don't have much experience driving pacers, but I know how to care for them, and have had some experience with them. I have a job in the works with the riding school, but I can easily tell them 'no thanks.' I'd definitely rather work for you."

"And I'll certainly give him the highest recommendation – about Mike's commitment and work ethic," Hans said encouragingly as he laid a hand on Mike's shoulder. "He's a natural with horses, and he performs all of his jobs in an outstanding way."

I stared at Hans with an open mouth. I was so surprised about what he'd just said that somebody could have knocked me over with a feather.

"Don't look like that, Sara," Hans said, smiling at me. "Mike and I were on the outs, but we're friends again. Both of us were stubborn, but it's all over now."

"But why can't he stay on with you, then?" I asked, but Mike shook his head.

"Hans already hired a young woman. I'm a little too heavy to break in the young horses, so he'll get more out of her."

"Well, if you want the job here, it's yours!" Eric said, smiling at Mike, who said okay! And so everything was resolved!

A while later we drove home, and Hans let both Mike and me off at our farm.

"Don't forget to clean the horse trailer later," grumbled Hans in his usual manner, but Mike just laughed at him.

"Aye, aye sir," he said with a joking salute. "I'll get it done, but first I'll just see Sara home."

"Okay, see you later!" Hans said. He waved at us, and then drove down the road to his farm.

We went out to the horse pasture to watch Fandango and the others. We couldn't see the horses until we went into the pasture. They were standing half asleep in a grove of trees in the huge summer pasture. Fandango raised his head and looked at me with his big, dark eyes and then he whinnied loudly.

"Listen to that," I said happily to Mike. "He whinnied. He hardly ever does that."

"He's thinking that you're the world's best girl," Mike said, putting his arm around me. "And you know – I think so, too!"